A Different Direction:
7 Possibilities for Saving the (Barely) Living Theatre

A *Different* DIRECTION:

7 POSSIBILITIES FOR SAVING THE (BARELY) LIVING THEATRE

JOHN AHART

LANGDON STREET PRESS

LANGDON STREET PRESS

212 3RD AVENUE NORTH, SUITE 290

MINNEAPOLIS, MN 55401

612.455.2293

WWW.LANGDONSTREETPRESS.COM

ISBN - 978-1-936183-19-7

ISBN - 1-936183-19-6

LCCN - 2010932957

COVER DESIGN AND TYPESET BY NATE MEYERS

PRINTED IN THE UNITED STATES OF AMERICA

Dedication

A book drawn from a lifetime of work owes an enormous debt to hundreds if not thousands who have made the experience possible. It is sometimes difficult to know who was most helpful in our choosing a better path when the direction was not so inevitable, who kept us going when the challenge was greatest. But these six people certainly played an invaluable part in my own journey. Night after night, for nearly all of twenty seasons, they were a welcome part of our efforts. A retired schoolteacher, a retired postman and his dedicated partner, a Midwestern small-tavern-owning couple and their disabled son.

In 1976, when the Bicentennial was about to begin, we named our company The Great American People Show. As the celebrations continued it was not always comfortable to be associated with others who chose that prefix for their shoe sales and barbecues. But these six dedicated and unlikely contributors made clear the name was appropriate for a theatre company created to bring to life stories from our country's core.

I can safely say of every one of the actors and crew members who came to be part of our work—no matter how erudite might have been their beginnings nor how rewarded their creative efforts before or after—not one of them left without feeling they were blessed to have had the friendship and dedication of these six incredible American People.

They knew very little about theatre's history, little about the Broadway and London scenes. But they knew about life. And they shared that knowledge through banjo playing and bonfires, through lemon shakeups and Sunday morning brunches. They shared it with homemade chili dogs and chocolate-cherry cakes. In return, they made clear they loved the stories of America that were told again and again by the actors who came to work in this remote corner of Illinois. Actors who often looked not at all like them.

And we all changed because of it.

—So here's to Margaret Ford, to Bud Faith and Irene Bennett, to Phil and Imogene Rebbe and their son, Paul. Here's to you—our own, great Americans.

Contents:

Introduction:

I wrote a book on directing—a textbook. It was published in 2001, three years after I retired from teaching and six years after I gave up my theatre company. It has thirty-five chapters and three hundred forty-four pages, and writing it gave me a chance to reprocess what I had learned and how my own thinking had changed over a forty-one-year career as a director and teacher of directing. Surely that was enough.

And it was—for six or so years.

I went on to other things. To writing, with my wife, a book on relationships, and to grandparenting, also with my wife, to cite but two new obsessions. And because I moved to Los Angeles I began to pay more attention to film than to the theatre. Oh yes, we still went to the theatre. Occasionally. We even stayed past intermission. Also, occasionally.

But if it hadn't been before, it now became vividly clear to me that theatre—the living theatre—has gone the way of opera. It's for the diehards. A fringe art at best. Pretty clearly inconsequential to American daily life, and for most who work in it, or at least try to work in it, a potential stepping-stone to something that might really pay off: film or television or Cirque du Soleil or video games or rock concerts. A stepping-stone to something else. A stepping-stone to something where, at the end of one's career, one can feel it has been worth it. A stepping-stone to something more in tune with the culture.

Don't get me wrong, I loved the theatre. I loved much of what I had had a chance to do and passionately believed in what the theatre could be. I think of myself as extremely lucky to have had the opportunities I've had. But it was enough. I was tired. I had fought the battle and lost. And now that I had quit, it felt good to go on to other things.

But my wife wouldn't give up. And so we talked about it. We talked about it every time we saw a play and I was coaxed by someone to say what I felt about the evening. I tried. I really tried. I tried to be polite. I tried to be generic. I tried *not* to be one of those voices I had resented so, three or four decades earlier. I tried not to be one of those early peers and colleagues who seemed never to be able to enjoy anyone else's work, who spoke bitterly of the winding down of their own efforts and how you couldn't find the right actors anymore, or the right script, or the right audience. But I didn't manage it well. First I was silent. Then I would try clichés of semi-approval. And finally, I'd hit the soapbox and off I'd go. And somewhere in the middle of reshaping the world I'd hear myself and try to make a graceful exit. There were sometimes voices of appreciation, of course, and sometimes I might let myself actually hear them. But mostly I would resolve again to "go on to other things."

So how did I get *here*? How did I get back to the keyboard with the hope that someone—several someones—might somehow take a chance and dive into these thoughts with me? That some of those people who are still trying, still in the system or bucking the system—people still trying to make it happen—might actually risk reading about changes *they* could make?

That was the crux of it.

It was easy to find critics—fellow travelers who might decry the lack of great theatre. (I think it's easy, although I haven't run into too many of them lately. Acceptance, perhaps? Indifference?) What was likely to be much more difficult was finding people who would actually risk reading about possible changes for themselves—changes they might consider for their own theatre practices.

"The system survives because it serves the people who are a part of it." (That's what my wife would say. She's an organizational consultant. A very good one who goes into dysfunctional organizations and works miracles—at least for a little while. Amazingly, people thank her and invite her back. And sometimes the changes that come about actually last.)

"So *if* I wrote such a book," I thought, "—if I wrote such a book addressed to the stakeholders in the system…" (*stakeholders* is a word it wouldn't have occurred to me to use before our marriage ten years ago) "I would have to believe change is possible. I would have to believe people who are profiting from the current theatre system in America might still be willing to consider changing the only part of the system they control, their own practices."

Maybe.

Maybe, but always difficult. Whatever the system. And in the theatre…? One only had to look at its history since the mid-twentieth century.

To raise the quality of theatre, directors would have to change—to me that seemed obvious. Even experienced directors would have to change. For I believed directors were at the center of the system. Yes, I understood the role of producers in the power game; I knew about the primacy of the playwright; I recognized all it took to make theatre happen was an actor and an audience, and that "the star" could sell tickets as no one else could. But when it comes to the quality of the theatre produced by our so-called modern system, all roads run through the director.

Yes, I know. The director can't, and doesn't, do it alone. But a good director, a wise director, makes nearly everyone's contribution better. And an incompetent director, an unseeing director, stands like a landslide in the middle of a mountain road. It's sometimes possible to get by and go on, but the obstacles are enormous and the footing is treacherous.

I also believe established directors are a rough, tough audience. They do not easily give up what they know.

Change. It does not come easily.

Experimental—the word rang in my ears. I remember being startled when I overheard a young actor I had hired for my company during one of its last years. She had been speaking to a friend about the way we worked. She was excited, very positive—and then: "…he's very experimental!" I knew it was intended as a compliment, but off I went. Whatever came next, I didn't hear. Nearly forty years of thinking and observing and learning and teaching and directing and writing and stuff I now took for granted and had been practicing for what seemed like forever, stuff I had taught for years and found unquestioned by most of my students who found it pretty self-evident—all this was *experimental*? Different from *standard practice* it might be, but for me it sure wasn't experimental.

And that was when a simple but profound realization set in. I had come to take certain practices for granted, and yet for most they were still questionable. It wasn't the way it was done. Not what others expected. Not what actors expected. Not what designers expected. Not what they did in the real theatre.

Yes, I've written a different kind of textbook for training young would-be directors. And it's become reasonably popular, certainly more so than I feared when I was trying to find a publisher. But there are a lot of directors who are already "trained," trained in the sense that they have learned whatever their "director training" had to offer, much of it very different from my own best experiences and my own most valued beliefs. And not only do these directors produce much of the theatre that most agree is undergoing one of the longest death scenes in human history, some of them are also teaching what to many has become an unteachable subject: directing. If big changes in the system are to be in the forecast, they probably aren't going

to come from those who believe the system got them to whatever level of success they enjoy.

So we talked about this would-be book—my wife and I—
and, meanwhile, I continued to do other things.

And then a bunch of little things happened:

A Thanksgiving in London—was that it? Was that really
the beginning of enough hope that I was willing to try again?

Or was it the audiences at Ashland?

A lousy *Mother Courage* in New York? (No, not *that* one.)

Lincolnesque at San Diego?

Lunch with Larry, who had spent a long passage of his life
at the helm of the Kennedy Center?

Listening to a passionate reformer of opera?

When there has been a lot of disappointment, when dreams
are lost and one goes on to other things, it's not easy to resume
the struggle. Not that temptation doesn't visit, but it passes.
Maybe not so easily when we are younger, but at seventy-three
it passes.

And my trump-of-trumps: I had been there. In my soul-of-
souls I felt I had found it: had known what it was the Greeks
had talked about when they created the Western theatre. For
twenty years I had a theatre company where I experienced
it. It was not always perfect, of course, but time after time it
amazed me. I envied no one. And certainly no other theatre.

I had considered writing a book addressed to theatergoers about how their need to have it all amount to something
might rescue the invalid if they better understood what they
were asking for. And it might. After all, don't most recognize
bad films when they see them? Why *do* they tolerate a quality
of acting in the living theatre they would walk out on if seen
in a film? But theatergoers are in short supply. At least theatergoers who aren't attending to support their actor-friends or to
support   daughters-who-can-sing-and-dance-better-than-the-
ones-we-saw-on-Broadway are in short supply. And to mount
significant pressure on the system, don't you need more people
to care? More people who haven't already chosen something

else? And then it occurred to me: To change a system where fewer and fewer people care, don't you need to get to the players at the center? The ones who will be the last to leave? Yes, for one who had spent most of his life as a director, it seemed obvious I should write for directors, experienced directors.

But there was more. If real change was to come, wasn't the starting place writing for those who cared deeply enough to want theatre to be better? Who still believed in the *possibility*, even if they less and less frequently saw it realized? Didn't it start with anyone who might be open to new possibilities? Who might be willing to see a different direction? Even directors couldn't do it alone. No matter how insightful they might be, no matter how insightful they might become, any core changes brought to the system would have to be welcomed by everyone: by actors and designers, by producers and playwrights, by board members and audiences. They too would have to see and welcome the difference.

But the final concern and, in all honesty, the one that had probably held me back from undertaking this project a long time ago, was: Would the people within the system—the ones who have to make those changes—listen to a retired seventy-three year old who had spent his working years tied to the *academic* theatre even as he headed his own theatre company?

There was a time when my own productions could be seen, when the quality of my own work might have been offered as a possible testimony. No longer. Yes, I had had my own theatre (called "an American Treasure" by at least one critic), had directed well over a hundred productions, had taught directing to graduate and undergraduate students for forty years, had written a bevy of plays for production by our company at a unique site in a unique physical theatre, *but* I had chosen to stay outside the world of "professional theatre," as most in America defined it. I had chosen not to compete for the obvious prizes. No Tonys, no Oscars, no Obies, not even a Jefferson on my resume. They didn't hand them out at New Salem, Illinois.

"Show me the money!" they would say. So.... I went back to other things.

Besides, at about that time a much more important and profound issue was dominating my concern: I had become obsessed with the organizational morass that had led to the war in Iraq. "The other things" I had been doing for the past six years had been dominated by my reading most everything I could get my hands on about the Bush administration and about America's military intervention in the Middle East.

And then, in early 2007, I read Barack Obama's *The Audacity of Hope.*

I was impressed. More than impressed, I was grateful. He had been honest—or at least so it seemed to me—and he had repeatedly spoken what I believed to be the truth: To get ourselves out of this quagmire, to regain respect in the world and have a chance of moving the world toward a more productive, peaceful future, leaders had to speak from the heart and they had to be immersed in a genuine compassion for all peoples. It seemed to me Obama was able to write about that so well precisely because he was born outside the circle and because he kept processing this system that he came into, not as an inevitable inheritor, but as a near alien.

No, I didn't know if Obama should be president of the United States, nor even if I would support him in the coming election. I only knew that he wrote a book that struck this student of the American Experience as an important reminder just when we needed reminding. It spoke to me. It spoke to one who had been asking, as I think many were asking, "How in the world do we get back in touch with the best of who we are? How do we return this nation to something we can be proud of?"

And—somehow—*this* got me to the premise that writing a theatre book with a chance might be possible. Maybe such a book could become an instrument for change *if* the timing was right and *if* it spoke the truth—including the truth not only about what I was saying, but the truth about how I came to say it, about how I learned it. Just maybe I could get some clarity for myself and for the reader by remembering that I would not have learned what I have, nor believe as I do, had I been more deeply entrenched in the system. From outside the system, I had learned what would have been oh so much more difficult to learn had I been more willing to play the game.

Yes, it might be difficult to get those who are/were part of the system to listen to one who had chosen not to play the gone-to-NewYork-to-earn-my-fame-and-fortune-in-the-theatre game, but whatever I had learned, I had probably learned it precisely because I *wasn't* immersed in meeting the day-to-day demands of that system.

And suddenly I realized: It was true. If I had gone to New York back in 1957 when I returned from Korea and my two years in the U.S. Army—if I had set out on a career in the "professional" American theatre instead of going to the University of Minnesota for a PhD—I would have missed it. Even in Minneapolis–St. Paul, I would have missed it had I tried and succeeded in becoming part of that first season of the Guthrie Theatre as several of my fellow classmates had done. (An image came back: I was in Minneapolis to see the plays in that inaugural season of the Guthrie. It was near the end of the run and I had gone backstage to talk with my friends in the company; the conversations were so negative, the morale so low that I came away stunned by their distrust of the future. Here they were, finishing a season in that long dreamed of theatre—the one that was to usher in a means of breaking the commercial/Broadway domination—and it seemed as if most of them were anxious to get away. To move on to something else.)

As for me, I went from grad school to a tiny liberal arts college in Ohio, where I soon began the real education of my life, directing two shows a year, designing three shows, teaching six classes, heading a department, creating a flexible theatre in a large former classroom, and listening to an audience hungry, as it turned out, for a chance to see plays by Jean Giraudoux, Thornton Wilder, Samuel Beckett, Ugo Betti, Moliere, Anouilh,

Durrenmatt, Wilde, and Shakespeare. And the die was cast—or
at least half cast. For that led to my returning to the University
of Illinois just when they were about to open the Krannert
Center for the Performing Arts, christened by the *New York
Times* "the Acropolis on the Prairie," where shops and designers became available to help mount productions the likes
of which few professional companies attempt. And that led to
my starting my own theatre company drawing on stories from
American history, a very different company, with an opportunity to learn from evolving new systems so unlike those that most
commercial, resident, academic, community, and summer-stock
theatres were experiencing that some might even call it *experimental*—no matter how I thought about it.

Yes, that theatre of mine was exhausting, filled with its
share of disappointments and plenty of frustrations. But, at
its best, the experiences were amazing, for audiences and company members alike. As subjective as I knew I was, at its best, I
would have welcomed comparisons with any theatre anywhere.
Anywhere.

So I began to write.

.

Prologue:

A confession: It's rare, but when I see theatre that's really good, I cry. And if it's great, I sob! It's embarrassing, but I sob. I fight back as much as I can; I try to choke down the sound of it; I struggle to cut it off so as not to make a spectacle of myself—but it's about as near to that uncontrollable edge as I can get. And in that rarest of rare productions, I sob and I laugh uncontrollably.

There. I've said it.

I'm not sad when I cry at the theatre. I'm delighted. It feeds something deep in my soul. It's how I know I've not succumbed to total skepticism, how I know there's still a glimmer of hope for the theatergoer in me—as restless as my legs usually become and as often as I turn to my wife and ask, "Do you want to see the rest?" We're on the way out at intermission when that happens, of course, and she knows it's coming and she will usually say, "Well...I'd kind of like to see how it plays out." And sometimes I'm glad when we return, because the second act *can* be better than the first. But I'm not a patient and generous theatergoer.

I do not write this with pride.

I've seen a lot of theatre—a lot of bad theatre and some very good theatre. And I have seen theatre that taught me what theatre can be. If you haven't seen that—well, I sometimes think that's the core of our problem. All too few—including many working in the theatre, I suspect—have seen what the theatre *can* be. At least, if they have seen it, it must have been such a rare, rare experience they were somehow convinced the gods had intervened. Whatever standard such a sighting might have set seems likely to have been compromised by the instant assumption that such quality is possible only in another place (London? Berlin? Moscow?) and in another time when finances were very different, audiences were very different, rehearsal time was very different—in short, when really talented people were working in a very different system.

Would you cry or laugh at the same productions I do? Maybe not. Not always. No two of us bring the same set of experiences to a production, after all. And your interests won't match my interests. Not exactly.

But if you believe, as I do, that the power of great theatre lies in its ability to connect us to one another, in its helping us share universal human experiences—experiences drawn from matters of life and death and the most significant struggles and celebrations in between—then most of the theatre that moves me deeply has a strong possibility of moving you, too. Tyrone Guthrie was thinking of something close to this when he wrote of the director as "the audience of one." It's a director's job to view the evolving work on a production as an audience might. And yes, I know, no two audiences are alike, just as no two individuals are alike. And sometimes it was quite clear to me that we needed to seek the "right" audience for our work; that it was too much to expect *everyone* to meet us halfway. But no matter how limited the audience, the theatre needs to more often expect *someone* to be deeply moved by the stories it tells. Several someones. If it is to survive, the theatre needs to raise its sights. It needs to stop settling for mediocrity. As Linda Loman says, "Attention must be paid."

No matter how polished, theatre trappings alone won't do.

I'm reminded of a faculty meeting called to discuss a production of Chekhov's *The Cherry Orchard*. We had taken on a
new theatre department head and it was one of his first directing efforts at our much envied performing arts center. We had
quality designers, excellent scene and costume shops, state-of-
the-art lighting equipment. For a college campus, our casting
pool was reasonably large with enough graduate students to
provide adequate maturity and experience. The new department head had had the pick of the lot, and when the run was
over he held a faculty meeting to discuss the production. There
was an extended exchange about many, many production elements and directorial choices and I alone had remained quiet.
As the session was winding down, my silence was apparently
obvious, and my new boss turned to me and said, "John, you've
been very quiet. What did you think?"

It was near the midpoint of my directing career, and though
I led the directing program, the new department head shared
the teaching of directing courses, had considerable reputation in academic circles, and was obviously quite proud of the
production.

I paused as long as I could, considered what I might say,
and finally spoke as simply as I could: "I didn't believe there
was a cherry orchard; I didn't think anybody left it; and if they
had, I don't believe anybody would have given a damn."

He was obviously and rightly startled, but no more than
I was when he replied, "Well! If you want *that*, we could have
given you *that!*"

He is gone now, and I have long felt bad for being so blunt
in my reply, but I have also never forgotten his response: "If
you want *that*, we could have given you *that!*" Today, I would
try to be more diplomatic in my answer, but the essence would
be the same. And if he—or anyone else—should suggest there
is another option when producing *The Cherry Orchard*, I would
recognize that we have a very different understanding of the
business of theatre.

Theatre can become incredibly complex. To mount and sustain a production, thousands of decisions have to be made involving the creative efforts of a human collective—usually a collective with widely differing experiences. Too often, the system reinforces habits and practices that work against quality. It is all too easy to look for answers under the current porch light when the lost keys are to be found under the trees, farther out—in the orchard.

If we're going to change the system, if we're going to pull the living theatre up from its mediocrity, it seems to me we have some serious searching ahead. Here's a list of seven possibilities for beginning.

#I: Search for the core of the story. RELENTLESSLY INSIST THAT <u>EVERYTHING</u> INCLUDED IN THE PRODUCTION HELPS MAKE THAT CORE BELIEVABLE AND SIGNIFICANT. ELIMINATE THE REST.

I put this at the top of my list, knowing you may think it obvious, question its validity, dismiss its language, or sneer at its impracticality—to say nothing of the possibility that you may just not get it.

Why persist? Because when the theatre is mediocre—or worse—it's clear to me that this possibility was never realized. If we don't get this one right, the rest won't matter. Of the seven possibilities discussed here, its successful practice may be the most elusive. But to achieve quality work that reaches the soul with any consistency, you must start here.

For several decades now, many of us—whether audience member or theatre professional—seem to have become confused about the essence of theatre. Of course, describing the theatre's essence may have *always* been an imprecise art, one more easily demonstrated than articulated. And yes, in our eagerness to demonstrate how strong the theatrical instinct, haven't we often interchanged the theatrical with the theatre? Haven't we included clowns and jugglers, pageant wagons and vaudeville, stand-up comics and shamans in tracing our historical journey? (And what exactly is performance art, anyway?)

But in the modern era, the modeling by two seemingly parallel and extremely popular art forms—novels and films—may have caused us to assume we have more clarity about the living theatre's core than we do.

All three—novels, film, and the living theatre—allow us to tell our stories. But what can be included in those stories and how we structure that telling differs greatly from one medium to the other. Some of those differences are obvious, others not so apparent.

Without a doubt, the contemporary theatre has benefited enormously from practices first introduced, or at least made widely familiar, by the novel and by film. Much of my own work borrowed extensively from the two sister forms. At one time or another, I've included narrative evolving into represented characters and places, multiple scenes, quick cuts between times and places, slow motion and a wide range of other time manipulations, to say nothing of an almost unlimited number of devices to provide settings and introduce and develop the backstory—to use the current film jargon. Add to that the demonstrated possibilities from mixing live performers with simultaneous video and audio images—live performers including not only actors, but dancers, musicians, and most anything and anyone else one can imagine—and one is tempted to argue we have long since accepted Wagner's theory that there are not many arts, but one. One art, and all the options are among its tools. In an ADD society, in a culture where nearly every child's (and most adult's) attention span requires a series of new and different stimulations if it is to be sustained for twenty minutes or more, why wouldn't we employ all the variants of the theatrical spectrum we can find if we want to amaze and delight our audience? What we have come to believe is this: Almost anything can be included in a play.

Well, yes, I suppose it can. In a general sense.

But in a more specific sense it cannot. Not if we want it to leave a powerful and lasting mark on its audience. Not if we want that living theatre experience to connect us at the most profound level. There are lots of toys to choose from, but be careful. In any one piece of theatre, be careful. And that's where the difference between the living theatre and its two very successful relatives, the film and the novel, deserves our cautious attention.

The film, by its very nature, is a highly edited medium. No one would consider showing unedited film as the final product if they are seeking a quality performance. The novel, on the other hand, may or may not be carefully edited (of course it usually is), but whatever the final product, it does not have to sustain our attention with the intensity demanded of the living theatre—it does not have to be consumed in one sitting to be successful. To state the obvious: We are used to putting the novel down and resuming it at our convenience. In the theatre, we can't leaf back through the past seven minutes to remind ourselves who Fredrick or Constantine is or why he or she is suddenly the key to the hero's past. In the theatre you have to stay connected.

In the theatre you need *these* words to be heard. The phone has to ring *now*! The mother *must* see what is exchanged between her daughter and the neighbor. The story isn't complete without each piece. It doesn't ring true. Its significance is, well, significantly dimmed.

Too much fuzziness, too much excess baggage, too many detours, and our attention wanders. We disconnect, the emotional ties are broken, our "internal critics" spring into action. We are no longer interested in the story being shared, but are focused on the devices used to share it. Other priorities set in: "When *is* intermission and what did I do with my car keys?"

Obvious, you say. Well, yes, but in every less than successful production, there is a lot of "stuff" that is neither believable nor significant and the attention of our audience wanders. Why? Why isn't it easier to protect our productions from the disconnect that comes during such times?

Maybe we let our fascination with whatever's new—after all, the very name, *novel*, originated with the search for unique ways of telling the story—lead us on a never-ending search for the latest storytelling fad, just as we've been fad-hungry in everything else we consume. Maybe we are seduced by our own cleverness. And maybe we've lost sight of the enormous editing power of the film that makes possible those high quality dramas (and comedies) when you have two, three, or four years to sift though every moment of performance after performance, of scene after scene to see which ones add to the final product and which do not. Which ones are just not honest. Which simply do not contribute to the core of the story—at least, not enough to risk their possible distraction. Maybe we forget how much of most films' explorations are left on the proverbial cutting-room floor.

It's no accident that even Shakespeare's texts almost never emerge whole when brought to the screen. In the great filmed realizations of the celebrated bard of Avon—as sacred as his words are—we have come to accept cut after cut in the dialogue. Given the opportunity to judge not only the need for any particular phrase or sentence in any given scene, but to choose when the same intent can be conveyed as well or better by lingering on the face of the listener, by a musical bridge, or by any of a hundred other devices any competent film editor takes for granted, great films carefully select their way to the story's best distillation time and judgment can produce.

Here's the bottom line for the theatre: Shouldn't we simply agree that film and the novel will almost always be more successful in telling our stories than will the theatre?

Maybe that's what most of us believe. The numbers seem to support that.

The theatre is a chancy business. Audiences make a difference. A single performer's having a bad day makes a difference. A blown light cue or a missing prop makes a difference. A forgotten line makes a difference. Even when we recognize the need for careful editing, even when we are trying desperately to see that those soft, fuzzy moments where the story seems to wander are somehow intriguing enough that the audience doesn't disconnect—even then, the living theatre has to accept that no two night's performances are ever exactly the same. It might have worked yesterday when the critics or my neighbors or Aunt Beatrice saw it, but what in the world happened tonight?

With the popularity of novels and films setting the standards, how can theatre have even a chance to compete for our interest? The obvious answer, then: It seldom does, and the American public knows it. That's why a lot more people read novels and go to films than see plays.

But there is another question and another answer. When do plays have a chance of competing for our interest? To be competitive, the living theatre has to be done extremely well. When that is true, the one advantage the theatre has over films and novels stands a chance of bringing the audience back again and again. So we have to be very clear about what makes theatre awfully well done—not hide from it when it isn't—and we have to be certain of the living theatre's one advantage (and it is its only advantage) over novels and films: *In the theatre, something* significant *has to happen*—here, *between us,* now! *It has to happen between these actors and this audience, here, in this place, on this night, now.*

On the very best nights, the audience knows they are a part of it. Because they came, because they attended, because the actors shared the story and the audience brought their memories—we *all* are able to feel the truth and significance of the story reenacted among us. Audience and actors alike feel it and know it counts. The electricity registers the worth of the event. None of us will forget. Together—in this place, on this night, we are connected by the power of sharing human experience.

To make that possible—not guaranteed, but possible—everyone involved in the production needs to know what is at the core of the production. Every decision made to rehearse the play and every decision made to support the production—costumes, setting, lighting—must be tested by asking, "Does it help make the core of this play believable? Does it help make it significant?" That core of the story must be so clear to all that when the inevitable distractions occur, when the concentration wanders, every single contributor quickly regains footing, finds a way back to the path, knows what he or she must do if that story—that dramatic action, that universal human experience—is to play out to its ending.

And what is that core? What is that core for *The Cherry Orchard*? For *Macbeth*? For *Lincolnesque* or *The Three Hotels*?

To get us all on the same page, someone better be able to name it. Somehow, if the collaborative art of the theatre is to realize its potential more often than it's doing now, someone within the production company needs to lead that company to a shared understanding of the core. It's possible the playwright can do that in the script. Maybe the lead actor can create a model so demanding that all will follow. But in the theatre that I know something about, it seems vital that the director recognizes that core and articulates it often to the many whose contributions will affect the final performance.

And how does the director name it?

She must distill the play into words that convey its universality. She must make clear that this play is about each of us who prepares the play and each of us who comes to see it. She must name the universal core that actor and audience alike will recognize as true and important. She must tell us what happens in the play and we will say, "Yes! That's it! That's a truthful and significant human experience and it affects me—when I am part of the re-creating of it, when I see it, when I hear it, it can affect me deeply!"

And for that naming, for that distillation, what are the choices? Two popular labels come to mind: "conflict" and "story." Both are used frequently and both have serious limitations.

One could certainly argue that actor training has dominated the preparation of the current generation of theatre people—directors included. And to the degree that any serious analysis of the essence of the theatre—of the dramatic—has been part of that education, the most common term repeated in theatre exercise after exercise, it seems to me, has been conflict.

Conflict as the touchstone for theatre was not introduced by acting teachers of the twentieth century. Critics in the late nineteenth century were responsible for that. And almost immediately there were numerous others who pointed out the many valued dramas where conflict was not central to the play. But conflict has been an easy concept to relate to the actors' scene work, to the actors' day-to-day analysis of lines and actions, and, one suspects, to an all too easy assumption about the core of drama.

The idea that conflict is the core of the theatre might well be true for a few dramas—there are plays about "the struggle," "the war," and "the battle," after all—but conflict is most useful not for naming the play's essence, but when considering tools that raise the stakes. If we are searching for a means to elevate the story's significance, one of the most often used is conflict. Because of conflict, the protagonist is not able to depart as he had hoped; because of conflict, the union takes a long, long time to accomplish; because of conflict, the confession comes out in small increments, with delay after delay and misrepresentation after misrepresentation.

Yes, there is conflict in most theatre, just as there is conflict in all our lives. But the core of most of the theatre's stories, just as the core of most of our life's experiences, is not conflict. We are trying to do something else and, yes, conflict gets in the way, causes it to take longer, delays the expected, heightens the tension—but, most of the time, it is not the core of what we were trying to do last year, nor for the last ten years. It is not the core of what we were finally, finally able to accomplish, and it is not the core of those dramas that tell the stories of those experiences.

So if *conflict* is not the essence, what is? More recently, led (at least it seems to me) by film analysis, we have been hearing a great deal about "story." Descriptions of "story" and "back-story" fill the papers as critics attempt to evaluate the success of major motion pictures, independents, and documentaries. The suggestion is that if we have a "strong story" or a "quality story" or a "relevant story" we are likely to have a successful production.

It is useful to remind ourselves how difficult it sometimes is to answer the simple question: "What have you been doing since I last saw you?" How many words do you need to get to the core of it?

In fact, what *do* we say when we try to tell someone the story of our experiences over the last ten years? And is it an accident that Americans pay therapists hundreds of millions of dollars—and perhaps more—each year to help them try to figure out what is happening in their lives? What is it you are really doing with your days, after all? And if we should want to make a play about it, what would be the core of that story?

There is a lot of detail that might go into the novel, and sometimes a great deal of detail that might be part of the film, but would that be useful as part of our answer to our awaiting friend who asks the question, poised as we both are, on a street corner, where we unexpectedly met? And what would we include in the telling of that story (however dramatic we know the past years have been) were we to bring an audience into our theatre for the two-hour re-creation of those events?

Aristotle was probably trying to get at all of this some two thousand years ago when he wrote of tragedy and the *imitation of an action*. Eric Bentley placed it in front of us again during my own graduate school days, when he identified "dramatic action" as the essence of the theatre in his classic work *The Playwright as Thinker*. But neither Aristotle nor Bentley was entirely clear about how we should distill that core of the theatre—that description of dramatic action. If they had been less abstract, perhaps we would be seeing better theatre now. Perhaps we would have more people laying down a template, using it to test not only their scripts, but the believability and significance of their actors and all that supports them, such as costumes, settings, sound, lights—all.

So how can we do better?

First, we have to believe that plays are about people. Not about settings or costumes or technology. *People* are at the center of the theatre. We gather actors into the circle and there we ask them to reenact stories about human beings and their worlds. About their life journeys. And we watch and listen. And if the core of the story is true and if it is significant, then all the embellishments must reinforce the truth of that story, must help make that story even more significant.

Moreover, the power of the best of these stories is that they are universal. The core stories are experienced again and again. They are never twice the same, of course, but never entirely different. And the audience that gathers in the living theatre watches those reenactments, and as they do, they bring their own experiences and match them up to what they see. On the basis of their experiences, they judge us. "Yes, it is true." (Or not.) "Yes, it is significant." (Or not.) And when it is true and significant—when it is at its very best—that audience responds in amazing ways, and those actors feel it and that community of actors and audience celebrates their rediscovering that life-truth together. Together they have re-created the only dimly describable. Together they have reaffirmed the theatre's power to help us share what often seems unsharable.

Together they have recognized that you too understand—not exactly the same, perhaps—but you too have been moved, you too have seen the absurdity of it, you too have seen the possibility, you too have gone through it and survived.

And those few universal cores for our stories—those dramatic actions (and there aren't many, fifteen or twenty, perhaps)—*can* be named and we can all recognize them. We *can* distill that core! And once we name it accurately, it can be amazing how many actors, designers, and stagehands have experiences that can be brought to bear—can be important tools in the collective creation of that time and place.

For me, that naming starts with acknowledging two simple universal realities: Each of us was born; each of us will die. These are the two universal acts in each of our lives—birth and death. They give us the first two fundamental distillations of universal key actions, of the core of stories that have served the drama since its beginnings: stories of birth and stories of death. So, we start with these two names for our distillations. And what are the others? What are the key dramas in between? Well, my experiences tell me there are many possibilities: My aunt's *marriage*? My wife's *search*? My sister's *discovery*?

And your neighbor's *concealment*? Your grandfather's *escape*? Your brother's *arrival*? Your uncle's *judgment*? Your father's *confession*? How many of those stories were significant enough to change a life? Might change any of our lives?

There isn't a limitless number of these universal experiences, these profound changes in our passages that send us in new directions.

So the most useful distillation for a production is to name the key action—usually only one, occasionally two (and in rare instances, three). The play *will* be about *the departure*—finally. Finally, they do leave *The Cherry Orchard*. And because of that, life for them will never again be the same.

And yes, other plays *will* be about *the birth* (sometimes we may call it more accurately *the discovery* or *the invention* or *the creation*). At their most basic, these will be the distillations at the cores of our stories. There will be variations, of course. *The death* may sometimes be more usefully described as *the murder* or *the suicide*. *The seduction* may be better seen as *the entrapment* or *the bribe* and, yes, you can, and eventually should, add details about how each character is connected to that core. But, in the beginning, that distillation serves us best when it is bareboned: *Macbeth* is about *the killing*—the killing of his friend and king—and *the search*—a man's search for absolution. *The killing and the search*—everything we do to create the production of *Macbeth*—everything—must help to make that killing and that search happen, to make them believable and significant.

And you must edit that production to exclude from the story everything—*everything*—that makes the core less believable or less significant. No matter how effective it was in last week's rehearsal, if it is does not contribute to the action's truth and significance, it must go.

As obvious as it sounds, all too many productions I see lose sight of that. All too often no one was able to distill the core of the story of the play—no one could name the dramatic action. No one could suggest how each character and each production element served to make that core ring more true and more significant. All too much in the play and the production hadn't been tested to be sure it counted, to be sure it was needed.

Essentials were missing; nonessentials were included.

And we disconnected.

. . . .

And then we left, wishing for what might have been.

Get the distillation of the core right and great theatre can happen. Not always, of course. Maybe the insights aren't there. Maybe it really isn't a story of universal significance. Maybe more skill and experience *are* required. Maybe actors or designers have to let go of old habits, have to let go of egos and fear. But, at its best, the theatre can be powerful stuff in leading us to a new understanding of ourselves. It's powerful not only because there are great scripts in our libraries, not only because we have a few great artists who work in the theatre, but because nearly every collective group has some amazing experiences hidden away, some gems of discovery from their own past lives. Given a chance, given focused, intense, extended efforts to experience the story outlined in a quality script, such a company is capable of producing amazing results. I, for one, have seen it again and again.

Yes, they may be too inexperienced and resistant to change, the rehearsal time may be too short, the script may be too obvious, but when we get the statement of the core right and all in the company bring their collected lifetimes of insight to bear, possibilities start to unfold that can surprise every one of us.

At their best, they may remind us what we have nearly forgotten: She's down, but she ain't dead yet, this living theatre.

#2: Make the cast's experiencing the play the primary goal of rehearsal. KNOW THAT IT WILL TAKE TIME AND MATURATION. KEEP THE STAGING OF THE PLAY SECONDARY UNTIL THE STORY BELONGS TO THE CAST.

Most plays I see are under-rehearsed. I am not referring to the support elements. In many theatres, advances in theatre technology have clearly resulted in more elaborate and more reliable technical support than was available only a few years ago. Lighting, projections, complex sound scores, and set changes usually glide by without a hitch—not a human hand in view, not a flat threatening to topple. No, it's not the technical support that has been slighted; in fact, those elements might serve as proof of the time and money invested if you're a playgo-

17

er questioning the ticket prices. It's the acting that has been shortchanged.

At its best, the theatre is a powerful tool for understanding, because it can share more than the logical, more than can be captured by the written word. By using the whole human being as its primary medium, the theatre, at its best, gives us an incredibly subtle and complex means of examining and understanding those events that happen to other people—*and* to ourselves. It helps us address those profound and troublesomely familiar questions, "Who am I?" and "What kind of a world do I live in?"

Through the theatre we can walk in another's shoes. We can probe the elusive. Why else would psychology, that science-based study of the workings of the mind, hold *Hamlet* and *Oedipus*, *Death of a Salesman* and *Waiting for Godot*, in such high regard? Why else would we credit great plays with making such a contribution to our human explorations?

And yet, if we examine the preparatory system dominating most of our theatre, if we examine our rehearsal systems, our work with actors—the primary icons in the sharing of these universal experiences—that work seems too often to concentrate on the mechanical and near superficial.

Three realities dominate most productions' rehearsal periods: First, a number of people have to learn new patterns of behavior that can be repeated each night the play is produced. For actors, that includes learning lines and blocking, clearly seen by many performers as their most demanding tasks as they begin their preparation. Second, a lot of disparate elements contributed by a lot of different people must be brought together into some kind of whole. And third, rehearsals seldom allow for enough time to do all we might like to do. We have to emphasize some goals and minimize or discard others.

So how do our production systems handle these needs? Well, for one, we typecast. We look for actors who have already "done it." We save time by expecting them to do about the same thing they have done before. Less evolution is required. (Many years ago, I remember hearing Tyrone Guthrie say one didn't need a lot of time to rehearse *Hamlet*; most of the actors you'd cast in the leads have played their roles before.) And when we can, we look for actors who know how to work on their own. Didn't we just read Robert Altman's description of Meryl Streep as "perhaps the smartest actor I have worked with?" "She needed not one thing from me," he said of her work in *A Prairie Home Companion*, "and in any case, no guidance, direction or suggestion I could have given would have matched her flawless instincts." (*Time*, April 30, 2006) Well...how many Meryl Streeps are there? And when was the last time you worked with her or her equivalent? And even if you had a cast of Meryl Streeps, do they come to the play bringing all the experiences they need to share this unique embodiment of the story? Don't they need to see, to feel, to experience one another in the "shoes" outlined by this script before they are ready to share that story?

And when, in the rehearsal systems of today, do the actors begin to experience the world of *this* play—experience it *together*? Experience it with *these* faces and *these* voices surrounding them, with *these* life experiences helping to inform each of them as they struggle to puzzle out what it all means?

It's probably no overstatement to suggest that for many productions, experiencing the life-core of the play begins only after all the more pedestrian memorization and "trying on" is over. And sometimes—all too often, one suspects—much of that experiencing comes after the play is in performance.

So what are the primary phases in most rehearsal systems?

We read and analyze the play together. We block the play. We run the scenes and acts with blocking and lines, working on memorization until we are "off book." We polish the scenes. (At least one recent popular directing text identifies timing as the primary focus of these polishing rehearsals. Another suggests it is the period when we identify those words that need pointing.) We run the acts and finally the entire play. We add technical elements. We have a dress rehearsal or two or three. We open.

What's left out? Let's look at that simple list again.

For some companies, reading and analyzing the play together is a single read-through; for others, it can go on for several days with shared discussions of the meaning and purpose of the scenes. *Tablework* is the name Harold Clurman gave to it, and the idea is practiced to some degree in most companies. We sit together and hear one another, the director shares interpretations, and others may or may not offer their own thinking.

Tablework helps us learn, much as most classrooms offer learning. But as most of us have discovered the hard way, it's one thing to sit at the table reading and discussing a battle; it's another to be in a war. It's one thing to read and discuss anatomy; it's another thing to be in the emergency room when the first victims of a disaster are brought in.

No one expects a would-be stock car racer to become a skilled driver through tablework.

Extreme examples, you say? Yes, but aren't most plays built around events that send our lives off in a new direction? Those events we didn't think would happen—not to *us*? At least, not like *that*.

To find out what it feels like to "be there," to be in the play, you have to pull on the boots and wade in. And in this swamp—in most swamps—the water doesn't quite feel as we anticipate, and there are things swimming by our feet we never expected. Before we make it to the other side, we probably will need several opportunities to repack our bags, take a different stick in hand, and try again.

So how did we get here? How did we get in this swamp, anyway?

Some of this may again be due to the evolving influence of film. It's still only a small percentage of film (and television) where actors have the opportunity for adequate rehearsal. Yes, one can argue that rehearsal is less important to film. Without the need to repeat the action tomorrow and for multiple performances after that, it's clear many of film's finest moments come from near-spontaneous impulses captured by the camera.

Nor is it uncommon for a film actor to be given a script only for those scenes he is in and never to see the rest. Then too, shooting scenes out of sequence because of location demands means he is often asked to play the last first. There's also that simple solution for memorization problems in the weekly series: cue cards. And how does the television actor find time for the maturation that makes a story hers when the script is introduced at the beginning of the week, reworked for the next two or three days, and filmed at the end of the week?

No, there is not time for deep, penetrating study here. (All the more reason to admire the best of television's actors and the most powerful of television's shows.)

But film and television systems probably shouldn't be held accountable for initiating most of the fast-food practices found in the living theatre. True, they may have helped to legitimize superficial acting, but much of the theatre's rehearsal system was well in place before television or even film became the model for so many actors. Much in the theatre's rehearsal system has been in place for a long, long time.

I first entered a directing class mid-twentieth century. Alexander Dean's *Principles of Play Directing* was new then. It was the first text devoted exclusively to directing and, in general, reflected the system for rehearsals that had evolved during the late nineteenth century and the first half of the twentieth century. It reflected the system for rehearsals I was introduced to as a young actor. There were challenges to Dean and that system in the next few decades, the most vigorous probably coming in the late sixties when names like Peter Brook, The Living Theatre, and Jerzy Grotowski ushered in very different alternatives. There had been forerunners, of course, but the rebellion of the sixties was like no other most of us had seen. Before long there were plenty of new systems being modeled and a spate of alternative texts published. But as the Vietnam War and the Berlin Wall became history, the dominant concern of the country turned from protests to investments. The theatre, too, seemed to return to "normalcy," reemphasizing older, seemingly safer, more practical systems. Improvisation was a part of the culture now, but limited mostly to comedy with Second City and its fellow travelers as the models. The theatre's exploring new ways to experience the material went the way of political protest. Yes, there were—and are—pockets of guer-rilla theatre. But if you wanted to mount a production and not engage in what seemed to many self-indulgent rehearsals with little performance payoff for the time invested, you returned to more conventional models. Efficiency and practicality—put that another way: *cost*—became the guidon. And yet, the real need, if we were to honor theatre's deepest capabilities, should have become ever clearer.

Haven't we learned a great deal about the human brain in the last fifty years? Don't we now know that different behaviors activate different parts of the brain? That different kinds of memory are stored separately from one another? Isn't it clear that we use only part of our mind when we remember cues and recite words? If we want to involve the *whole person* in the recreation of the core of our plays, haven't the studies of the mind made it clear we have to prepare our casts differently than we did a half-dozen decades ago?

In my own evolution as a director, that awareness was sharpened by the challenge of bringing to life familiar stories from American history—stories where at least the basics were known by nearly everyone in our audience. Where, it seemed to me, we had to share some deep-seated truth discovered by the cast itself, or we had little new to offer the viewer. That truth might be suggested in the words or the structure of the production, but it was more likely to be found in the seriousness of intent, the effect of the stories on the performers. It had to try to generate what Stanley Kaufmann memorably called "bonedeep truth" in the *New Republic* when he sought to ex-plain the appeal of Jerzy Grotowski's Polish Lab Theatre for America in that long ago fall of 1969. Kauffmann was writing of the Polish theatre's effort to dramatize the holocaust. We were aiming to dramatize events no less familiar.

As the artistic director for a theatre company that became the State Theatre of Illinois, I created a number of plays devoted to Lincoln and the American Experience. The specifics were drawn from primary sources: letters, newspaper accounts from the period, transcriptions of speeches, and journals kept by the historical characters themselves.

So who owned those stories? Well, in the most fundamental sense, the stories were owned by those who lived them. Of course, we couldn't be certain all the details we re-created were consistent with the original events. History is subjective, after all. But we tried. We tried to find the most widely accepted sources. We tried not to put words that were never spoken in the mouths of the characters. We tried to pass along the observations and feelings of those who had been there as best we could discover them. We felt a certain responsibility to get it right.

What was the model for our thinking—at least for my own thinking—about our intent? There were a number of influences that had seeped into my pores, I suspect. Certainly Thornton Wilder's *Our Town* had been one of them. To play the stage manager at sixteen as my first real experience in trying to enter into a quality script was something I revisited again and again over my years working in the theatre. I remembered those lines Wilder had written: "This is the way we were at the beginning of the 20th century. This is the way we were in our growing up, and in our marrying and in our dying."

To line up those chairs and imagine that cemetery on the hilltop had been—even at sixteen—very real to me. It had brought back images of my own childhood and a little white church on a hillside, the graves of my grandfather and my grandmother up above that church, and it had reminded me of the many lines of mourners I had seen winding their way up through those iron gates to stand among the gravestones and take stock. (And yes, we could see the Baptist church down in the hollow from that hilltop, just as we could see much of the life I knew as a child spread out in the fields before us.)

So Wilder's play had been more than fiction for me. It was about the world of my grandparents, the world they knew and the values they held. And to be a part of telling that story, even as a young man, seemed to call for some responsibility on my part. I needed to get it right. There was some truth there that my own experiences recognized, significant truth, and even as a young actor, anything I did needed to honor that.

But an ever clearer model for my believing that the story must belong to the cast may have come from a production I first directed when I was in my late twenties. It was Brecht's *The Caucasian Chalk Circle*. Like Wilder, Brecht did not base his play on any set of specific facts—it was a reenactment of an ancient Chinese parable, after all. Also like Wilder, he began the play with a storyteller, this time with a group gathered around him in the remote Caucasus Mountains. The storyteller seemed to be addressing who they were and how they came to be there. He spoke as if there were only a few who knew: a few of the older ones, perhaps. They were a people with threads to their past—a bit of the story passed on to one, an artifact stored away in a trunk by another. As we worked on *The Caucasian Chalk Circle* it became clear to me how important it was to have the cast develop a personal responsibility for owning and passing on the story. What if they *were* the only ones who knew? The only ones still living who had heard what it was like to have been there?

And so it was with our stories from American history: What if *this* cast—the people recreating the story *tonight*—were the only ones who knew? What if the sharing depended on them? What if this was all that had survived about the story of Lincoln? About the Civil War? About the struggle to end slavery? Incomplete as it might be, subjective as it might be, what if this *was* the only story we had to pass along to the next generation? And what if we believed it to be the best truth we had, *our* best truth—and what if we were absolutely convinced of its significance in our attempt to understand ourselves and one another? What then? How determined would we be to find and share our best *then*?

An interesting thing began to happen: Audience members began to tell us of their response—not just their response to the actors or to the plays, but their response to history. Never mind that much in the plays was easily available historical material. What they said was, "I learned more history tonight than in all my years of schooling." They spoke of being "deeply moved." One professor of history wrote, "You are sharing *felt* history." They cried as we told of Lincoln's body being brought back to be buried. They shared with the cast their own stories passed on to their families by someone who had somehow been touched by the St. Louis race riots, by Hiroshima, by the battle at Gettysburg. They told us their own memories of the Great Depression and the bombing of Pearl Harbor.

How did that happen? How could even scholars of history be moved by young actors presenting the story of Lincoln, by that first demoralizing retreat from Manassas? How could they be moved by the burning of the Bonus Army camps at the Anacostia Flats, scattering those depression-hungry World War I veterans who had marched to Washington to demand what they were promised—a dollar for each day fighting in the "war to make the world safe for democracy"? How could audiences sob at the death of Lincoln—now more than a hundred years past—as a small chamber orchestra played before them, three young narrators recounting the long journey home as they lit candles in the very room in the Old State Capitol where his body lay on the dais before them, the dais "...strewn with evergreens and white flowers." Sitting in the original chamber of the House of Representatives, some in the seats where Lincoln and his colleagues once sat, some sitting in the balcony looking down on that scene—they sobbed. Sobbed for a death now nearly a hundred and fifty years in the past.

I began to realize this was the theatre the Greeks had given us—this communion of actors and audience. I began to understand at a different level why our actors had to enter into the plays if they were to share them, had to experience for themselves enough of the truth of the events to bring the audience into the circle with them. I began to understand that they had to become a repository for the "truth" as best they could discover it, and that the performance was a sharing of their truth with an audience that came to celebrate that communal history together, bringing their own understandings and the learnings that had been passed along to them. I began to understand that those experiences—however complete or incomplete they were—would be used by each of them to test the stories we were reenacting. Together, we would—each night—see how truthful and significant our *felt* history seemed to us, actor and audience alike.

The importance of all this to the making of quality theatre might never have solidified for me were it not for those twenty years of directing for that theatre company.   It was only after I began that work that I realized the tremendous difference between short and long performance runs. In fact, early in that effort, I remember thinking, "We all know how to open a production; what most of us have had very little experience with is sustaining a production through a long run." To withstand the manipulations and battering of egos that come with extended public exposure—the commentary of critics, friends, and well-meaning and not-so-well-meaning audience members who are more than willing to offer their suggestions for improvement— is an almost impossible task for any company without frequent collective sessions to bring the whole back to a shared agreement about the play's core. I saw how absolutely essential it was to try to repeatedly bring all the performers onto the same page in their understanding of the play and to connect each of their roles to that core. Only if their understanding was rock-solid did they stand a chance of sustaining continuing performances of the same story we shared as rehearsals ended.

I suddenly realized why the Berliner Ensemble had used a very different rehearsal structure those many years ago as they sought to bring Brecht's epic theatre to life, why they

were able to take the post-World War II theatre world by storm
when they brought their work to Paris and London. (Time—
that was their trademark. Time for maturation. They rehearsed
until they were ready. And everyone was invested in the discovery—simultaneously. There were knots of actors here and there
working on this moment and that, so much so that American
visitors reported they often hardly recognized it as rehearsal at
all.)

I understood, too, why those American road show companies of complex productions seldom come close to recapturing
the most successful originals as they repeat the staging of even
brilliant choreographers. Staging and memorization are not
enough to capture the heart of the story. They never were. Only
when you own the story, only when you know it to be your best
truth, only when you need—desperately need—to share it because it's important to performer and audience alike, only then
will you have the possibility of great theatre.

I, for one, find most rehearsals I walk into shockingly like
the rehearsals I knew nearly sixty years ago. It may be a startling generalization for some readers, but I would say that
today, most rehearsals are dominated by fear:

Fear we won't have lines memorized.

Fear we will forget cues.

Fear that blocking will be sloppy and the audience will
say it looks messy—"amateurish" is probably the word feared
most.

Fear we will run out of time for bringing it all together.

(Oh yes, and unless we have a good sound system and lots
of body mics, fear the audience will tell us they can't hear.)

Our aim is to keep the play moving and keep it looking
slick. The words get said, the blocking repeated—extend that
to include the songs are sung and the dances danced—but seldom is the human being fully tapped.

How important is the actors' making the play theirs in
this system? Well, it may be desirable, but time and focus for

its accomplishment are largely the responsibility of the individual actor. Rehearsal? There's not a lot of time for collective discovery.

In fact, what assurances do we have that most directors could use the time profitably if they did declare experiencing the play the first goal of rehearsal? Is it possible that one of the real reasons most productions don't spend more time making a stronger connection between the story and the actors is the obvious one: namely, too many directors aren't sure they can do it no matter how much time is available? There are familiar examples that might lead us to that conclusion. One is the production company that endlessly runs the show through rehearsal after rehearsal. (I once knew a respected summer musical theatre that rehearsed its productions for six months—yes, that's six *months*—with almost all of that time spent on complete run-through after complete run-through of the play.) Another is the production that uses retro exercises from the sixties to "develop trust" and company rapport, but when the actual work begins with the script, returns to the same time-pressured system with little transfer of insights to enhance the actor-character connections.

All directors have models for connecting the actor and the role. It has been almost three-quarters of a century since Stanislavski was introduced to America, after all. But we all know it's one thing to say we are going to help actors better experience the play and another to get it done. Some of our models may need to be reexamined, just as our rehearsal priorities may need to be reconsidered. A possible first step is to recognize weaknesses in the current system that, if changed, might introduce opportunities for more promising work. Those weaknesses seem to me to be concentrated in two places: the repetitions we practice to accommodate rote memorization of lines, and similar repetitions to fix movement patterns—to "set" blocking.

In short, maybe our repetitions not only consume precious time unnecessarily, but cause us to memorize in ways that make it very difficult to involve the whole person in the experiencing and sharing of the play.

Here's the first truism worth considering: To have great performances, actors must make the language of any play's world their own. Yes, we have to understand what the words mean. Yes, we have to remember them. But, more importantly, rehearsals can give actors the opportunity to discover how saying these words—and hearing these words said by others—can affect how we think and how we feel, can affect what we do. Like a child discovering the possibilities for speech, we discover when words used can fend off intruders, when they can bring help, when they can connect us to another, and when they can disconnect us from another.

Rehearsals can provide opportunities for the cast to discover when the silence should be broken, when what is heard demands a response.

How? How do we do that?

I have come to believe we can best get there not by careful extended analysis—as useful as that may be—not by deciding intellectually how the words should be colored, but by setting up simple rehearsal situations where language *from the script* can be used as often as needed. Where silence is allowed, and speech comes only when useful or necessary. Where we learn primarily by *doing—by experiencing. By experiencing the interaction possible using these words as we share again and again with one another.*

We can give actors permission to take lines out of sequence and to repeat them, and to use those lines again and again in subtly different, but meaningful, ways. Not artificially manipulated sounds or words, not improvised lines, but phrases from the text intended for meaningful interaction with the characters who are logically part of that scene. Not long, extended lines, but phrases—verbal gestures.

Using the circumstances of the scene as the base, we can encourage the actors *to be there*—be there for as long as it takes—and when the impulse is to speak, to allow it to happen, repeating as a child might: "*Why?* But *why?* *Why* does he? *Why?*"

The only requirements are that it be language written for the character as part of the play and that it is spoken now as the actor listens to the others, demands from the others, and responds to the others. There must be real connecting interactions, real listening, and real responses. Words must be repeated until they are heard and have become meaningful to the speaker and to the listener. Words must be repeated until the repetition gets us what we need. Words must be spoken aloud again and again.

Language building is an essential task if actors are to experience the play. It's how the character's way of thinking and speaking become one.

Yes, of course, we will go back to the more conventional running of scenes with lines in sequence as we develop the scene. But we can bring to that work a recognition that the rote memorization of cues—as important as it often seems—can become a distraction separating us from our best impulses. We can learn that we speak because the *character* needs to speak. Rehearsal can become a time when we are not afraid of silence. We can make the words that are used the *direct* outpouring of our thoughts and feelings. We can learn to speak with the play's language as our language. We can stop being translators.

I found it invaluable to introduce again and again periods where actors were free to use whatever of the text's phrases and words were most in need of being said *now*. Words spoken in response to the place, to one another, to the time of day; words spoken to make the transition into the play's world at the beginning of rehearsals; words used as a means of discovering with whom they most needed to connect now, how important silence was now, how they *felt* now.

That's the key, isn't it? How do we feel *now* and what does that make us say or not say? If you doubt it, watch a young child who has not yet learned to disguise feelings and short circuit impulses while expressing needs.

It's probably fair to say that of all the unconventional techniques I came to rely upon, this was the one practice I found most helpful in leading actors to experience the play. Again and again, when rehearsals would become unproductive, when a scene brought only auto-responses, I would stop, have the actors gather in a quiet space, ask them to find simple ways to relax—to sit or lie down with their eyes closed, perhaps—and wait until they were ready to speak, and then to speak words and phrases from the scene. Words triggered by the faces around them, by the place, by the silence or the memory of yesterday. And as they waited, as impulses grew greater, out of the silence invested connections almost always began to evolve, taking us back to the world of the play and its connections.

It became a time for connecting at their own pace, in their own way. A time to use whatever route into the play was possible for them now. A time to be led by whoever was first ready. A time to wait until the actor's own mindset was ready, until words came, and until listening brought a need for action. From there it was often a simple matter to get them back on their feet and to resume the work we had intended for the session.

I made many startling discoveries growing out of the work with language development. For example, there was a period where we rehearsed a trilogy of plays in preparation for opening on three successive nights. These three plays were chronologically related, the first beginning with Lincoln's birth, the last ending with the moonwalk. To my delight, I discovered that the actors profited enormously by creating sessions where they were free to use the lines from all three plays interchangeably. Using their impulses to speak and respond, they created very logical dialogue between characters who lived in different time periods and never actually spoke to one another in any of the three stories.

How was this possible, and why was it important? They listened—really listened. The language became *theirs*. They began to see its power. They saw historic issues as recurring ones.

I learned that the strongest validation of an actor's work often came from peers. Toward the end of rehearsal, or well into the run of the performances, I would ask the actors to use these same practices with one exception: Now they were to speak anyone's lines but their own. With no preparation other than silence and the presence of the others, they would begin to speak. Memory of what they had heard would begin to dictate the choices. One phrase would trigger another, spoken and repeated, answered again and again. Words telling each he had been heard and remembered. Telling each she was important.

No matter how small the contribution might seem to the audience, to the fellow actor, these words were spoken here—now—because they had become an essential part of the play. Now, at this moment, they were among the few, best-remembered pieces of the experience. The result: smiles—validation—seldom shared at such a basic, affecting level for an actor's work.

And finally, here is the other perhaps equally important tool I believe is rarely fully appreciated as we seek to connect actors with the play: To experience the play, actors need to work in a stimulating environment. They need a supportive atmosphere—one that supports the work itself and one that supports the story they are trying to enter.

Just as we do with rote repetition of lines, we spend too much time with repetitions of the production's director-dictated physical form. We do this at the expense of time spent to stimulate impulses leading to the discovery or confirmation of the *best* final form. Rehearsal time is too often extended through repetition even though it isn't what the actors' impulses tell them they should be doing.

I learned early how valuable it was to ration actors' exposure to a very complex multi-level architectural setting so we might focus on the core of the story and not the challenge of remembering entrances and exits and the specifics of blocking when they were not yet ready. Conventional wisdom to the contrary, it's not always—one might say, usually—an advantage to have the realized set design for the opening rehearsals and all those that follow. I say this with absolute conviction, having revived one production with significant cast changes seventeen times over seventeen seasons—yes, seventeen! Alternating work off-stage with on-stage rehearsals, just as we alternated work with lines out of sequence and scenes as written, we sought to make the core of the play so familiar the actors could not only master a very complex script and stage, but could easily adapt to exporting parts or all of the production to very different performance spaces: think the floor of the Chicago Board of Exchange, think amid the artifacts of the Chicago Historical Museum, think on a paddle-wheeler at the New Orleans World's Fair—with only a few hours devoted in each case to restaging.

Yes, there are times when the cast needs the isolation and quiet of a conventional rehearsal room, but the other side of that coin is that few environments can be more sterile than a rehearsal room unless you make a concerted effort to create a supporting atmosphere in its space. The environment where actors enter into the play, where they try to experience the play, has a tremendous impact on the work. As rehearsals progress, the space will need to be modified. The cast doesn't always profit from having the set and props of the final production as they rehearse *tonight*. They need only that which helps them discover another level in their own relationships to the story's core.

I consider myself fortunate. During much of my career it was easy to take my actors to different environments. I could radically change atmosphere in a single evening—certainly from one night to the next. I have taken actors everywhere: into the woods, up stairs and ladders into bell towers, to the park, to the shore. We have rehearsed in the gravel, in the dark, in the rain, riding up and down elevators, on the tops of buildings...in the bowels of buildings.

Why? Always, the intent was to find a place where the connections were easier, more likely, and more inevitable, and where it became easier to connect the actors with one another, the characters with one another, the actors with the story, and the actors with that special time when the unexpected happened, the time when the inevitable happened. Always, we sought to make it easier to find out what it was like to walk in those shoes while being *there*—there in that place—at that time with those people hearing those words. What it was like to be there together in the silence. What it was like to need to reply—to *really* need to answer, to shout back.

Why? Why would I do something others might easily dismiss as experimental? Because that's the way it has worked in my life. Words have been said, relationships have changed, things have happened—because we were there. At that strange time we were *there*.

The link between the place and the words provides a powerful tool—a tool sparked by our own memories. Because we were in the right place at the right time—because we were in the wrong place at the wrong time. The place where the unspoken could finally be spoken. Where it was spoken—ready or not.

In my own experience, to give actors the chance to be together in such a place, hearing the silence broken by those particular words—repeated phrases cued by silence and sequences never heard in the play but real nevertheless—led again and again to the discovery of self, to the discovery of the connection between actors and between moments, connections unlikely to have been found in any commonly practiced repetitive rehearsal system.

That seemed as obvious to the actors as it was to me.

I cannot imagine directing *Godot* without going to a remote desolate place where nobody comes and nobody goes—where it *is* awful! (Yes, I remember taking them to a particular park with a particular tree on a particular hill where no one was around to share that world but us. And I remember taking them under the stage to the pit where in the darkness below the lifts for the elevator apron we worked in the shadows with echoes of our voices coming back to confront us.)

And no, I cannot imagine directing *Our Town* without going to a hilltop cemetery with the wind blowing in our faces and the clouds passing by in the sky above. And sometimes it was that obvious a choice, but at other times we walked the rails, balancing as we stepped past the ties, the gravel crunching when one misstepped, Gogo and Didi walking side by side—with me trailing along behind.

Yes, of course going to another environment was sometimes impractical. And sometimes we simply needed the quiet isolation of a rehearsal room or the familiar floor of the stage itself under our feet. But even then, to create light and shadow, to play music in the background, to work on a rug or a mat with the actors able to reach out and touch one another was often what produced the first significant breakthrough. It was followed by breakthroughs on which the rest of the rehearsals were built, which were made possible by the use and modification of the space, even when we knew full well the action of the play in performance would call for distance and weapons and armor or any one of many other barriers to such obvious connections.

Whether it was Brecht or Shakespeare or stories from American history, to have actors walking through the trees, stretching out on the forest's carpet, hearing voices coming out of the darkness, climbing the ladders, climbing onto the roof to see who was out there—any or all of those moments helped to create a new world where the play was possible. This cast began to know a shared world, where the core of the story seemed more immediate, one might even say real—where it seemed true and important.

If actors can make the language their own, if they can have repeated opportunities to enter into the story in environments that support the core of the play, if, together, they can sense what it feels like to be part of the action of the play—happening and significant—that collective ownership of a story, that experience, is ready to be shared.

Is there time for all this? Time in any system of rehearsal we can envision and support? Well, it depends on how often we are challenged by the possibilities, how often we see our work as the descendant of a two-thousand-year-old discovery passed down to us by the Greeks. Yes, I know. That sounds preciously academic to some. But suppose we just say, "It depends on how often we aspire to create theatre approaching the quality of *Sophie's Choice* or *Brokeback Mountain* or *Casablanca*." And now we're back to aiming higher.

The point is this: High quality doesn't demand pretentious-ness or even a traditional subject or style. It only demands that the work digs deep.

To strive for the best theatre can offer may begin with no more than an awareness that you can't fake honesty. We know that about our best novelists and our best filmmakers. At the core of both there is a bone-deep truth. If the theatre is to share our most enriching human experiences, those who are central to that sharing have to know what it is they bring.

Rehearsal—it's a time for finding out. We can use our time and energy more wisely, and we can find more when we need to.

We can choose bone deep over slick—if we are willing to change the system.

To those who say there's too little time and not enough money, I ask, "Could you do it with more time and more money?" Maybe you need to find out if you can. And if that begins to happen, maybe you'll find you can get better at it. Maybe the memorization will come more easily. Maybe the blocking will be more obvious. Maybe the actors' life experiences will enrich the play's moments in ways that are hard to describe, but make all the difference. Maybe if you are more insightful and more skillful, maybe if everyone in your system expects to work to-gether to create those experiences, maybe *then* the time and the money required will be less than you think. When actors own the story—own the core of the story and it is deeply a part of them—memorization and blocking can seem relatively minor obstacles.

That's what often happened for me. In fact, I was often saved by having less time and less money. We became more cre-ative because of it.

What would that be worth to you?

#3: Pay close attention to modules of time—the building blocks of <u>every play</u>. USE THEM TO SHAPE YOUR REHEARSALS AND TO DEVELOP THE FORM OF YOUR PRODUCTION. USE THEM TO KEEP FIRST THE ACTORS AND THEN THE AUDIENCE ENGAGED.

How long is the ideal theatre performance? Are some plays just too long? Some too short? And are most of us better at preparing some length of plays than others?

Experience provides an obvious answer: Absolutely.

Some plays seem too long for most in the audience—sometimes *much* too long. And, yes, occasionally, some seem too short. We're just getting started and it's over. Of course, that changes. It can change depending on whether it's Tuesday or Saturday night, whether the performance starts at 3 p.m. or 8 p.m. Whether we are on vacation and have traveled a long distance to get to London or Ashland or Stratford or whether we have driven downtown, finally found a parking space, and know the kids' babysitter wants to be home before midnight.

Many of these factors seem beyond the production's control. One isn't: We can do our best to make sure the length of the performance is right for this story presented by these people.

Don't we always do that? Isn't that obvious?

What if we can best do that by trying to make sure all the parts of the story are given the attention each deserves, so the audience feels ready for whatever follows next, and the next after that? What if the scoring of the play leads inevitably to the climax and the ending comes when we are ready for it, and afterward the audience is sent out into the night knowing they have experienced the whole, whatever the play's length?

When we do that well enough, can't the three-hour play whiz by, and even if the babysitter awaits, isn't it possible we will know this is a rare experience we wouldn't want to cut short under any but the most demanding of circumstances? Isn't it possible we wouldn't want to miss it? Not a minute of it?

Recently, the theatre has, seemingly, "discovered" or at least popularized a new theatre form: the *ten-minute play*. As I write this, Google offers twenty pages of listings for "Ten Minute Plays"—97,300,000 entries. There are several annual Ten Minute Play Festivals, and at least one is now in its eighth year. One is tempted to say, "The ten-minute format is sweeping the country!"

…for now.

It probably doesn't matter that the Futurists of Italy and Russia not only wrote manifestos urging the theatre to get in step with the new world of acceleration and speed as long ago as the beginning of the *twentieth century*. It doesn't matter that they wrote and published three-act plays requiring only a page for their printing, and even shorter plays that purported to be "complete" but contained only two or three lines of dialogue. (The motorcycle was a favorite icon of that brave new world, and who had time to sit for more than a few minutes when there was so much to see, so much to do, and all these new machines for doing it?)

Today, one might argue, our attention spans are even less forgiving, so it is probably not surprising that ten-minute plays have found an audience. Not surprising, but when presented, most of the performance offerings feature several such plays. In fact, "Ten Ten-minute Plays" is a common format. So, it may not be that we prefer theatre in smaller doses; maybe we just think ten-minute plays are easier. And for most, they probably are. Easier to write and easier to produce. And if you don't connect with one—well, here's another.

I think we often suffer from trying to make theatre easy. The best is seldom easy and never obvious.

It sounds a bit crude and condescending, but I think some who produce theatre are in the player-piano business. Of course, it's easier to recognize others' low expectations than to recognize our own. I continue to be amazed that public television, one of the most aspiring outlets of all mass media, still runs an occasional You-Too-Can-Do-It painting program complete with specially cut sponges and shaped trowels as the artist before us demonstrates how you can create a landscape just like his. Never mind that the paintings resulting are all too much like those available in Kmart or at the corner lot's truckload art specials.

To create real art you have to see. Really see. See the difference. See what is special, and work to distill it until it's there to be shared by many and maybe even most. Each of us has some special sensitivity for seeing and some special tolerance for sanding—for keeping at it until the form emerges. To create great theatre requires no less. The question is where to direct our effort.

When it comes to the seeing and the sanding of the theatre, I know of nothing more challenging than working with time. One might go so far as to say, in the temporal art of the living theatre, it's our ability to shape the building blocks of time that requires the greatest effort and the most acute sensibilities.

And now we're back to the ephemeral nature of the living theatre and the indisputable fact that there is only one chance to make all those connections during the time of *this* performance, and when we miss—it's gone. That moment is gone. That scene is gone. That act is gone.

In short, this timing thing, this duration, this length business is very important. And it's not just the play's final length that's important, but the shaping of time in every scene—all the ones that seem too short (and underdeveloped) and the ones that go on forever (and keep us from caring about the next).

It's my belief that too often we give time only a passing blow. We fix the obvious in the moment. (An old graduate school professor of mine once said he was always glad when someone mispronounced a word in a speech. It gave him something to offer as criticism without fear he would make the speaker worse.) We do a lot of the little things: "Turn to look out the window when you say that; hit that *yesterday* reference a little harder." And we attend to the whole: "The second act is too slow; it's just too slow. Pick up the cues! Get ready—pick up the cues!" "More energy. From the very beginning—more energy! Make it special!" (A memory comes back of a cast member's story: how his director responded when the actor desperately asked for help in rescuing a comedy that didn't seem to bring laughter. The advice? "Be funny.") We tend to focus on the smaller pieces—a word here, a line there—and on the big picture—the act, the whole play—but too often we neglect the careful shaping of the key working parts: those medium-sized blocks in between.

For any of the arts, I've come to believe it's often the shaping of the parts that makes the difference. Most plays can best be explored, rehearsed, and realized by dividing them into units of about two to three minutes each. I cringe when I see the implied certainty of those numbers. And I hasten to add: It has nothing to do with counting—and yes, there will be exceptions, some shorter, some longer. No, I've never used a stopwatch to determine the value of any given length of time. (Thank goodness, unlike television, the living theatre doesn't have to fit its work into precise time blocks.) It has to do with our attention spans. Ours—the actors and the director, as we work to discover the play—and those in the audience, as they seek to connect the play with their own experiences.

I discovered that in my pre-rehearsal analysis of the script, the one thing that again and again served me well was to divide it into units. I ended up with forty to forty-five rehearsal units for a full-length play, again and again, script after script. Over a long career, the numbers were nearly always the same. These were not timed divisions, but divisions determined by the changes in what's happening in the play's script. Changes in the mood of the play, in the dominance of one or another character in the story, and in the play's action. Those script-dictated changes determined my building blocks for creating any whole production. In a full-length play of about two hours, an intermission included, that suggests two to three minutes for each unit.

Again and again much of my work on a production was with those blocks of two to three minutes of performance time. In rehearsal we might often spend an entire evening on one or two of those blocks. Why? We all have limits. We get tired. Mental fatigue sets in, for the actors rehearsing and for the audiences trying to connect. We can take in only so much and then we need change. Change too often, and that too can cause us to disconnect.

In each of these blocks we came to somehow instinctively feel the sense of the whole, where it started and when it needed to come to an end. We knew where we were. As we worked we began to more fully understand its relationship to the whole.

We put it back into a run of the longer scene or act to test our assumptions.

When actors have made key units their own, when the work there becomes truthful and carries out its function in making the play's action happen, the whole production can be changed—significantly. Why should that surprise us? Just as in our personal lives, to achieve clarity in any one of our key relationships can bring significant changes in our family inter-actions, at our office, with our friends, or in the community.

I believe that only by coming to see these working units— these time blocks—as the most fundamental determiners of the play's score will the director (and the actors) be able to easily move from one production to another preparing *any* play, no matter what the length of the whole.

The difference between working on a ten-minute play and a two- or three-hour play can be enormous. By learning to shape the play's units, to fit them to the whole, we prepare ourselves for the scoring of any production, whatever its length.

In our everyday life, we take for granted the value of di-viding the human body into its several parts. We do the same with our machines, whether they be automobiles, computers, or watches. We do it with the preparation of our foods. In almost every task we undertake, we recognize the value of understand-ing how the parts are related, the value of seeing each smaller piece as it affects the larger unit. The two-hour play is simply too large to hold each of its many parts—each line, each move-ment—in our minds as we try to find out how each needs to be shaped in relation to the whole.

It's not that most directors haven't paid some kind of atten-tion to dividing the play into scenes. Rehearsal schedules will attest to that, with "Tonight we are rehearsing Act II, scene 3…"—even when the script is not episodic and the playwright gives no indication of scene divisions. And by now, most—not all, but most—directors have recognized the limitations of di-viding the play into scenes based on the characters' exits and entrances. So some version of unit divisions plays a role in most rehearsals, and the term "beat" is a part of nearly every actor and director's vocabulary.

But from what I have observed, most directors haven't yet become convinced that the living theatre performance must be as carefully scored as a symphony—I would even argue that it must be *more* carefully scored than a symphony, because there is no conductor out front to bring the actors back together when they stray.

Performances are built in time. The challenge is to know when one block ends and another begins, when each should reach its climax, how each relates to the unit before and the unit after, how it relates to the whole, how the rhythm and tempo of each sustains our attention and moves us through the play's events—how each of these blocks must be shaped and put into its proper place if the whole is to achieve the level of significance we seek.

If that seems too detailed, too demanding, I would ask you to consider a complex piece of sculpture: Rodin's *Burghers of Calais*, for example. Which of those twelve hands, those twelve feet, those six faces could have been created without careful consideration of the others, without knowing how each fit one of the six figures and how that figure contributed to the whole of the six? And if that is obvious for this piece of sculpture frozen in time, is it not even more true for plays, where we are dealing with faces, hands, feet—all—as they move through time after time after time after time?

Some scripts are extremely difficult to direct well without careful attention to these time divisions. No play has made this more obvious in my own experience than *Waiting for Godot*. Long ago, when it was first published, I had difficulty even reading to the end. I have now seen it performed many times by experienced and even acclaimed actors, and seldom is the production successful in keeping me engaged. In contrast, I have directed it twice and the rehearsals were among the most enjoyable of all my efforts with actors. What I remember best was the little that was required of me as a director once I had carefully divided the play into units, identified the line which seemed to me to best capture the essence of that unit, and arranged the schedule so the actors could focus on one or two units at a time. My memory of the experience is how free I was to simply enjoy the actors' discoveries. Does my memory mislead me? Is that really true? Of *Godot*?

Most recently I used *Godot* over a seven-year period in rehearsal classes with young actors and directors. Contrary to what a friend of mine asserts, I believe there are very few, if any, actor-proof plays. But I was again delighted with the results. Working on carefully defined units, a wide range of actors made the scenes believable and arresting again and again. No small accomplishment for this work that is still mysterious and avant-garde in the minds of many.

When we begin to see the importance of shaping a given unit, we can quickly test the changes we make in a particular moment. Small changes *will* affect that unit. We should be able to sense that. We can tell where each moment is in relation to that unit's beginning and end, and how it affects the mood and each of the characters in the unit's action.

We run an act or the entire play to see which units need attention. We give our most concentrated efforts to the individual units that have the best chance of affecting other units around them. We reassemble the act to see how our units flow as we move through the larger sequences of the action.

In a sense, the work on a full-length play is akin to painting a meticulously detailed but enormous mural. When we step back far enough to take in the whole, the detail is difficult to see. We have to sense how the whole will come together in time, but we have to work on each part to do the shaping each demands.

The complex scoring of a production emerges not from hard and fast paint-by-number rules—although there are some obvious rules we have all learned, sometimes from others, sometimes from experience—but from subjective decision after subjective decision. (Even our choice of following one of those "rules" or not following it is a subjective judgment.) Those multiple judgments are so complex it would be foolish to argue that everyone can learn to score a play brilliantly any more than one can argue that everyone can write a great symphony or challenge Rembrandt's skill in painting portraits. But what we can suggest with confidence is that to give focused attention to the shaping of these modules in time and to the structure resulting from putting them together one after the other significantly increases the possibilities of creating richer, more powerful theatre.

Anyone who has taken a course in playwriting has likely had an instructor who called attention to the spelling of the word *playwright*. By definition, we speak of the writer for the theatre as the shaper of plays. But it is not only the playwright who is a shaper of plays. The actors and director (and in the best of worlds, the designers as well), working to develop a score for the use of the words, the emotional involvement, and the movement patterns, are also shaper of plays. Together, these collaborators develop the score of the production. They too are playwrights.

At times the effect of extended work on a given scene can produce results for the whole act, sometimes the whole play, that are only a little short of miraculous. Relationships suddenly fall into place. The tempo and rhythm for the entire play begins to sing. The actors' energy is doubled, their concentration and focus sharpens. I've seen it happen again and again. Magic! Why? Because when the key block is understood and shaped, when it becomes theirs, the rest of the play suddenly seems so much easier to sustain, so much easier to drive to its climax. Where before the action of the play seemed to drain the energy of the actors as they struggled to unlock its secrets, now the play's actions energize them. Somehow their bodies and subconscious minds understand. They have broken through the barriers.

To make this happen, the director needs to have instincts that lead to two early definitions for each time block: first, its title, and second, its beginning and ending lines or actions. The title given to the block should set the direction for the work. It should constantly remind the cast that, though there may be many, many words in the text, and many specific complex actions to be mastered for the two or three minutes of this part of the story, all of it can be distilled to fit under this umbrella. In my own practice, the words that best provided that distillation came from the text itself. Sometimes that's easy. Sometimes it's a search requiring multiple readings and even patching together two or three phrases to make a succinct distillation reminding all involved of the dominant characters and the essence of the unit's action and its atmosphere. It answers the question, "What does all this add up to in the context of the whole play?"

We know where we are. We begin to see the direction we're headed in the discovery: "He cried. Cried to me. That boy—that boy is going to be magnificent!" Just reading Willy Loman's words as the unit's title we are reminded how emotion-filled this familiar block from *Death of a Salesman* can be. Here is where we learn why Biff comes home. This is the time when we see Willy finally—finally!—realize his worst memories can be purged when his lost son accepts him. Forgotten? No. Forgiven? Maybe not. But accepted. Accepted and still loved. With sensitivity and sanding, we can begin to try to enter into its truth. We begin to shape the block of time that propels us toward the play's finish.

Sometimes we can start the work on such a unit early. Sometimes we must wait until we get in place other, more accessible sources of discovery. Other blocks. Sometimes we find a rehearsal hitting a wall. And then we look for the key, the place where we are unable to play the truth. That's the block that must be attacked until we find the answer. To unlock its mysteries becomes the challenge for all the rest.

To find the right words distilling the unit's essence tests the artist in every director. There are no guarantees. More than once I have spent hours working on a unit only to decide that as logical as it seemed to me, my time block was too much for the actors. They couldn't get from beginning to end without "sitting down to rest." Their minds were overloaded with too much history, too many words or physical demands that were too new and too complicated. Again, the near miracle can happen. It certainly did for me in every one of those instances I can remember. By breaking what had seemed like a perfectly logical time block into parts *a* and *b*—sometimes parts *a, b, c,* and even *d*—and working with each of the new divisions separately until each was shaped and owned by the actors before going on to the next, what had seemed baffling now seemed eminently manageable. So simple, it seemed like magic.

Time—it's at the heart of the artist's work.

This is probably most evident in the creation of original works, particularly works with complex structures and extensive reliance on musical underscore and physical action. Much of my own directing during the second half of my career was with just such efforts. Time and again, there was no way one could evaluate which scenes were successfully carried by the text and which needed the underscore or the physical action without rehearsals to shape the scene. Some scenes that appeared successful on paper were discovered to be overwritten once they were in rehearsal. Others that appeared to need additional text development could be carried by the personality of an actor. It's the shaping of the whole scene, block by block, that tests the mix.

Man of La Mancha is a well-known script that is less than perfect in the reading, but in a well-scored production is a powerful theatre piece. Farces with their demand for invented, complex physical action, musicals where plot is embellished by dance and song, one-person plays where the actor's fatigue and loss of concentration can easily allow the piece to wander outside its intended path—*all* are familiar forms needing careful attention to scoring. In fact, there is no script I know that can't profit from mindful, sensitive shaping of its units—be they many or a few. Be it a short play with a small cast or an epic with a large cast.

We begin with a blueprint—sometimes an idea. Together we explore, discover, create, distill, and edit until each block is formed. We shape each to lead inevitably to the next. No two directors will shape a production exactly the same. No two casts will allow it to be shaped exactly the same. What belongs and what doesn't? What should be developed, what condensed? What given less time, what allowed more?

Time. For the living theatre it's fundamental. Yes, there may be rules: Ones you can evolve, a few others may pass along. But mostly your choices come from your own insight and experience. You have to listen—and see. Like any art, you have to use your best insight, and then do it again and again, working to be more efficient, more precise, more penetrating—again and again.

One of my favorite artists was Albert Hirschfeld. (Few of us remember his first name. We knew him as just *Hirschfeld*. In his drawings the extension of that name was Nina—his daughter. It was her name that he managed to conceal in his drawings, giving us a numerical clue to the number of times her name appeared.) Hirschfeld was a brilliant caricaturist. His drawings of American theatre luminaries appeared regularly in *The New York Times* for more than a half century. Each persona was captured with such economy and grace, each with accompanying involvement in the energy of a life-filled moment, that many of us retain his images years after they were first published. He was an artist who never acted or directed a play, never wrote a script, but was so beloved by Broadway a theatre there is named after him.

How do you teach someone to do Hirschfeld's art? Well, you don't. Not exactly. There are a few, I suppose, a very, very few who might challenge his economy in capturing on paper the essence of a human being invested in life. But not many. Hirschfeld had an amazing eye. He was able to see the essence of a person's image, and how a few—only a few—well-drawn lines could capture it all. "That *is* Ethel Waters," we would say. "That *is* Carol Channing." And he did it again and again and again. No matter how intently we try, how patient we are, few of us are likely to match his results. What he saw was unique.

Great theatre comes from what the artist sees best. From strengths. From the best sensibilities shaping the blocks that move us from beginning to end.

I love great folk art, art born of the undeniable need to sing or to dance or to whittle. Great folk artists speak for their people. For their children. For the celebration of nature. For the victims of war. In fact, might we not say all great art is folk art? We may begin by learning the skills that have gone before, by studying the historical best, by listening to the mentor; but to evolve into the truly great artist, every human who seeks to create will have to find their own way. Each of our standards may be unique, but I believe we develop as we more mindfully focus on the possibilities. Isn't folk art built on just such a premise? Don't naïve artists who produce amazing works get there by being attuned to the possibilities without worrying what the textbooks or the critics say? Art requires a safe place to learn—and encouragement. We can learn to better follow our own sense of time, our own sense of truth. We can better sense when a block is ready. When it will send ripples of improvement to all the others. When it is fully shaped.

When I was a young man, Edward Steichen put together a wonderful photographic exhibit he named *The Family of Man*. It brought together the best of images from photographers working all over the world. Arranged to follow our common life journey, it included depictions of birth, childhood, work, meals, lovers, weddings, parenting, funerals, hunger, war, religion, governance—multiple images of each drawn from cultures scattered over the seven continents.

First exhibited at the Museum of Modern Art in New York City, I saw it in one of the few intact public buildings standing among the rubble in war-devastated Seoul, Korea in 1957. It was unforgettable. For me, as a young American serving in the US Army, to see it as I walked among weary Koreans—children in formal school uniforms, women in traditional peasant dresses, old men wearing tall conical hats made of horsehair, all intently studying the faces before them—was indisputable testimony to the possibilities for sharing what at first seems unsharable. I took my own photographs that day. Photographs of those who stood studying the broad panoply of life depicted in that exhibit. One hangs on our wall even today.

The published collection of Steichen's *Family of Man* photographs included a forward by Carl Sandburg and was shot through with lines drawn from the world's poets. "Clasp the hands and know the thoughts of men in other lands..." (from *The Mood of an American Ship* by Nelson Collins), said one page. Around the words circled a dozen and a half photos of dancing, singing life. From France, Israel, China, Peru, the US—the people in one photo were dancing together in a circle with a bombed out building in the background, others were in the midst of a cemetery, and still others were in a city park at night, lights burning overhead.

My copy of *The Family of Man* is worn and taped together now. I have shared it with many, many actors as we started our work on a new play. Any theatre person who doubts the potential appeal of an artist's best work, whatever their style or cultural background, should find a copy of *The Family of Man*—it's still in print. To me, it's a vivid reminder of the communicative power of the human being.

That's the wonder of theatre: At its best, it's working with the most powerful of media, that incredible, flexible, subtle, arresting tool, the human being when he is most filled with life. Our job is to shape the blocks that allow those alive human beings to connect firmly with each other, with their journey through the events in a universal story, and with the audience that comes to see it.

Every block counts. Time building upon time. Shaping the journey to the whole. With care and sensitivity we can feel when each of those blocks is ready to be put in place. There are no cookie cutters for the best in theatre, no paint by numbers.

It's an art.

An art where we build a world in time. And then it's gone. Disappeared. If the best of theatre has the possibility of changing us forever, the artist knows how careful the work must be to build it. How insightful must be the choices. How determined must be the effort.

Block by block.

#**4**: Create your own, not someone else's, theatre. EVOLVE YOUR OWN STYLE, DRAWING FROM YOUR BELIEFS AND PASSIONS. KNOW YOUR LIMITATIONS AND VIGOROUSLY EXPLORE YOUR POSSIBILITIES.

Style—so simple and yet so complicated. So familiar and yet so elusive. Style—a personal viewpoint, a harmony of choices. Style—chosen elements brought together to make a whole, a harmonious whole.

And nowhere is style more important and its harmonies more difficult to achieve than in the living theatre.

Why? Because every production requires we play god. Yes, I know. There is more than a little hubris implied in that assertion. But the truth is, every time we create a production, we must build a world. Let me repeat that: To create theatre we must build a world—all of it. We must decide what belongs in that world and what does not. What in that world is known and what is yet to be discovered.

In that world, we must decide how people behave, what supports their lives, what makes possible their actions. We must decide what conventions will be acceptable for time's passing, for people aging, for violence that if real would maim our actors. We must learn what can be used to suggest structures impossible to put on stage, for weights and intensities too much to bear, for distances too far to travel, for spaces too expansive to capture. We must learn what will be acceptable as human connections that have evolved through generations of experience—familiarities that have been forged through the sharings of day after day, year after year. We must decide what people in this created world know about each other and what that information enables them to do or keeps them from doing, how quickly they respond to one another, and how readily they take up their challenges.

We must build a world where the play can happen, where it can be believable and significant. Where the audience is encouraged to bring their memories to meet us.

It's an enormous task. As we begin production work, we often take refuge from the challenge by suggesting the theatre is an "interpretive art." We imply that someone else has already answered most of those questions—and maybe someone has. But lest we become too infatuated with the insight of the originating playwright and the secondary roles of all who follow, think for a moment how seldom in today's theatre playwrights turn into successful directors for the scripts they've written. Not that it can't happen, but that it seldom happens is a reminder that writing the quality script is a strong beginning, but only the beginning—the beginning of evolving the production's style and a harmonious whole.

No matter how we start, no matter what we have been given—no matter if the script or the actors or the theatre space were chosen by someone else—if we want to create quality theatre, none of those previous decisions by others can be allowed to obscure the necessity of our seeing that the whole made from new and old parts, the whole made here and now, is, well, *whole*. An uncontaminated, harmonious, working-together whole.

To best understand style, to clearly see the work necessary to create a truly powerful and unique style, it's probably most useful to follow a production's development starting from a blank page. That was certainly true for me when I attempted to create productions from dramatic real-life experiences—from historic benchmarks, some well known and some nearly forgotten, but all seldom tackled as the raw material for the living theatre. How, for example, could one put on stage in a single production the First World War, including the St. Louis race riots in that war's midst, the 1930s Depression, the rise to power of Adolf Hitler, the splitting of the atom, the bombing of Hiroshima and Nagasaki, the race into outer space—all that alongside appearances on the American scene by Jane Addams, Will Rogers, FDR, Joe McCarthy, JFK, Martin Luther King Jr., and Norman Cousins, and they, in turn, accompanied by voices remembering moments from their own lives as they watched Lindberg fly the mail overhead, struggled with poverty and job loss, dealt with shortages, rationing, two world war efforts, and other daily happenings made unforgettable by the framing of larger, historic events? What words would make up the script? What images, what events could we re-create? What scenes, what actions could be distilled and linked together into a two-hour performance by a dozen actors, even if they did have a fifteen-level stage and creative designers?

Today, most of us would say film offers the better medium for such work. In film, after all, editing may go on for years. We open living theatre productions in four or six weeks or, if we're really lucky, after a preview run of a week or a month as we try to hold off the critics to give us a chance to see what is before us.

How can theatre *ever* distill such complex material, how can it select from so many possibilities? Of course, there is only one answer: When we are driven to tell the story, when we need desperately to bring it to life, we can only do the very best we can. When we are finished we offer it as our best truth. Then we watch and we listen to see if it evokes for the audience that which we have found central to the action of our play. And when moments fail and we have the opportunity, we try again. We go back into rehearsal and resume the search. We rewrite when we can, we watch, we consider the possibilities, and we start again. We start again by taking a walk with an actor whose moment doesn't fit. We bring in new images to share with the cast; we call them all in for work on a scene that has slipped away from us. We start again with a new cast and a new season, determined that this time, *that* moment will not escape us.

Considered as a whole, the options for our own play stretching from the First World War to the moon walk were overwhelming. And yet somehow we created a production from it all—a living theatre production that for four seasons was performed to enthusiastic audiences as the final piece in a trilogy of original epic plays spanning 160 years of American history.

That experience and several others akin to it made absolutely clear to me how essential is the search for the harmonious whole—the whole where all the pieces belong.

Often in the theatre, we try to do things that are hard for us to do. Very hard. And when we attempt many of them, our ineffectiveness calls attention to itself. It violates the harmony we seek. It contaminates the style. In the familiar world of practical production preparation, *whatever* the complexity of the story, new script or old, elements that do not belong can stop the show. Contamination detracts no matter how small the cast, how simple the setting, how few the costumes. Moments unsolved *do* cause us to disconnect: A dialect coach wants the actors to follow her lead and speak as she thinks they should speak if they are from Belgrade—and what happens when the actors can't make that part of the harmonious whole? Haven't we seen it a thousand times? How often do plays that aren't about dialects become memorable for the jarring disconnects caused by a dialect? Or an actor whose effort at being seventy-two only reminds us that he isn't seventy-two? Or one whose vocabulary and speech rhythms are far from those written into the world of *As You Like It* or *J.B?*

It's easy to chase the brass ring. Broadway's preeminence may be less than it was a half century ago, but the productions of Broadway or the West End or maybe Stratford or Toronto still serve as the models. We not only seek to produce the scripts we see there, we seek to reproduce the productions. We try to match their costumes and their scenery. We wish we had all those lighting instruments.

We want to play with the big toys. If only we had a chance to do *that*. To create *there*. To work with *him*. To have *her* in the cast.

When we fail, what is our answer? We didn't have the right tools. Had we more money, more connections, more clout, different collaborators, we could have made it happen.

Maybe. Maybe a few substitutes here and there would have helped. Maybe a better actor in the lead, a better designer for the setting....

But style is more than that—more than acting skill, more than designers on the payroll. Style reflects who we are—as individuals and collectively. I believe the best, most affecting, lasting styles reflect the passionate beliefs of the key creators. They grow out of what one or more of us see as important and harmonious choices.

We need to ask a simple question: Is it *ours?* Is this *our* world—the world we know best? Is this a place where we can share what *we* know? Where we can present the truth as best we know it? Where we can best bring the core of *this* story—the play's dramatic action—to life?

Style is chronically susceptible to imitation. All children imitate some adult in creation after creation. Eventually, the children discard many of those preferences as they find what really reflects their own personal tastes. Yet, we're all aware of the marketplace's manipulations of us adults as we're told what jackets and shirts are "in" this year—what needs to be discarded from our closets to avoid the derision of others. Some of us take these fickle dictates more seriously than others, of course, but few of us are unaffected by changing fashions.

Style in art is no different. Models abound. There are always those who have gone before who catch our attention—inspire us. They make us aware of new possibilities. Some of those models become so important they provide a lens through which we see the world. We may or may not remember that those are borrowed lenses. And equally elusive, we may not realize when we have genuinely and firmly made those preferences our own—made them our own way of seeing.

It may have started with Brecht or Shakespeare, grad school or living in Paris, but now is it how we really do see? How we really do think? How we process our own worldview? This personal view, this honest, direct reflection of what we take in, is central to being an artist. It's a truism, isn't it? Art, true art, art with a capital *A*, reflects how someone sees—how she sees life around her. How he translates that experience seen—or heard or touched—as he re-creates it. As she reflects it on the page or with the sound of an instrument. As he paints it on canvases or hammers it out of blocks of stone.

The would-be creator—the would-be artist—makes choices. Inevitably. He tries to make choices that complement one another, that fit together. He seeks a harmony of choices, and we use labels of style in our effort to identify those harmonies chosen. We make up new labels as shorthand for quick and erudite references to an enormous variety of creations. We nod knowingly when someone speaks of the Restoration theatre or baroque music or classical Greek architecture. We praise a few for their sense of style and we condemn others.

I remember how startled I was when *USA Today* first began to run its front-page graphs based on simple surveys reporting our opinions on what seemed like everything from neurosurgery to astrophysics. Americans seem to have an opinion no matter how limited our experience or information. Our judgments of one another's styles are probably not exceptions. We seem to know what we like and dislike, whether or not we've given it much conscious examination. We can't always tell you why we like some things individually or don't like two things together. We can't always explain our chosen harmonies; we just know that for each of us some things seem to go well together and some do not. My wife tells me she just doesn't like the color olive—or orange: "Well, I like some oranges, but I don't like olive—and I certainly don't like olive and orange together!" Those colors won't appear together in any of her harmonies. The surprising thing is that each of us is likely to enjoy putting a few things together that the majority doesn't think of as harmonious. Those paradoxes are often so unusual and so distinct they become the hallmark of someone's style. It's part of that person's brand.

We're not dealing with *absolutes* when we talk about style or about harmonies, all the rules for aesthetics we have learned notwithstanding. We're talking about preferences. About a viewpoint that is unique to every individual.

And so, preferred style in the theatre, as everywhere, may seem like a pretty arbitrary business. And yet, in the theatre as in all the other arts, the best work will inevitably have a strong sense of harmony. The choices *will* belong together. They will belong together because *someone* will see that they complement each other. They work together easily. They get the job done. And if the production is successful, if it moves the majority of us, if it seems believable and significant to its audience, when we see that production we won't wish we had a different actor in a key role, we won't envy some other production's design or wish we were in a different theatre space. To most of us, the props will seem well chosen, the musical score will seem to fit *this* production, the costumes will seem to serve the piece well—not by calling attention to the designer or the materials, but by making the experience of the play more powerful, more believable.

And no, I don't think that happens often.

Where do we start? How can we get better at creating harmony? In my own education the greatest gift I received from any one theatre mentor came from Frank Whiting. "Doc" was head of the theatre department at the University of Minnesota when Guthrie made a national search to select a city for his theatre project. That "The Guthrie" is in Minneapolis is due in no small part to the influence of Whiting. I was newly married, just back from the army and a year and a half in Korea where I had somehow chosen the University of Minnesota—with access to very little information—over some dozen or so other colleges that had offered financial support for my beginning a doctorate in theatre. Minnesota's theatre program was clearly in transition. Even then, before Guthrie began surveying the scene, there was a sense the Minnesota program was growing in national prominence.

When I arrived in Minnesota, Doc was in Japan with a group of students performing as part of a USO tour. I soon learned that at Minnesota production dominated academic pursuit, that the average graduate student spent far more time acting or building than in the library or writing. I was not entirely delighted with the discovery. It was the pre-MFA era and the lines between theatre practice and theatre history and criticism were not so clearly drawn. I had had what I considered an exceptional and extremely practical undergraduate theatre education, and my master's study had introduced me to a wide range of theory and history. After my two-year military diversion, I was anxious to get on with my life, and I feared if there were too many production assignments I would have to delay reaching my self-imposed deadline for my first full-time university teaching position.

That first semester, I enrolled in two directing courses taught by Doc, one focused on production and another on script analysis. We began with substitute teachers and it wasn't until some four weeks later that Whiting returned to the country and appeared in the classroom. I can remember very little about the academic content of his classes. Little about any specific skills encouraged or taught. What I have thought about again and again was much more overriding and can best be conveyed in one incident: We were discussing approaches to producing the classics, and as Doc talked of the possibilities for directing *Agamemnon*, he cried. Cried as he retold the story from this two-thousand-year-old primitive tragedy. Cried as he talked about *Agamemnon*, for God's sake!

As you would expect, there was a substantial amount of cynicism among the graduate students in that class. Not everyone saw tears as profound commentary, not even tears shed over a Greek classic. But beginning that day, I began to see directing differently. By semester's end the lesson was quite clear: Don't do scripts you don't care about passionately. It's not enough to *stage* a play—creative work is too hard, the effort demanded too great, the sacrifice of time stolen from other life possibilities too much. If you are going to spend your life working in the theatre, be sure what you are aiming for counts—counts when measured by your own set of life values. It may not be well received by everyone, including audiences or critics, but be certain you'll never regret having tried. Over a forty-year career, that lesson learned served me well: Start with something you're passionate about.

Let me be clear. When a style evolves with a strong set of harmonies, when things reflect someone's carefully considered personal choices—whether in music or architecture, painting or the theatre—I believe many of us, probably most of us, will find it appealing. We'll respond to it. They may not be our own preferences, they may not reflect a harmony we would choose, but when it comes together well because *someone* really believes these elements belong together, believes it passionately and works long and hard at its proportions, at its timing, at its shades of meaning or its shades of color—tests it for truth and significance—my experience tells me it's difficult to resist. Walk through any quality art museum and sense your own responses to the enormous array of harmonies represented. A strong, considered viewpoint is hard to resist. Whatever the style.

It works that way in nature and it works that way in human creations. Almost all of us can be awed as we stand on the beach at Kauai and watch the sun set over the ocean. As we respond to all the colors and forms, the sounds we hear, all that touches us—the wind, the sand, the person beside us—we cannot but delight in the harmonies present in that moment. But we can also delight in the spectacular view from a mountaintop high in the Sierras. Nor will many of us be immune to the wonder of the ruins of Machu Picchu or the mosaic of rooftops as we look down from a cathedral tower in Prague. Intellectually, we all have our preferences, but do it well—bring the pieces together with harmony—and we'll respond.

Can we do it? Can we tap that essential for the artist: the instinct for creating harmonies? I believe we can. Consciously or unconsciously we are all accustomed to seeking a harmony of choices. It's a part of our life habits. We do it every morning as we pull our clothes from the drawer preparing to dress for work or play. We do it every time we prepare a meal or order from a menu. We look for pieces that go well together. The problem: Overwhelmed by the number of choices to be made, we often let someone else make too many of those key choices. We use one element because we think we must, and suddenly nothing fits. We try to imitate someone else's production style and it doesn't match our resources. We ignore that there are other possibilities.

Today—after all these years—we see an amazing number of conventions used that were evolved for the late nineteenth- and early twentieth-century proscenium theatre, conventions that somehow are too often repeated without question. (Yes, I'm thinking of *Waiting for Guffman* here. *Waiting for Guffman* and the thousand other cousins that most of us could name.) The realism captured by the camera—images of real people having real-life experiences—has long since established standards for believability not considered in the centuries of more poetic depictions of human beings interacting. Yet, whether we're producing Shakespeare or Sam Shepard, whether our theatre effort begins as poetry or prose, someone has to evolve the specific harmony for *this* depiction. Someone has to make certain all the pieces fit in *this* created world. Has to choose not just the label, but the way we re-create this universal story moment by moment. What conventions, what evolved style makes *this* action believable and significant—*now*?

Every production we create starts with an imagined harmony. The most obvious source of that harmony comes from our belief that the action of *this* script will be more believable, more significant if it occurs in *this* kind of world. That the audience with its expectations and experiences will be best able to enter into this world if we create in *this* style. But what is important to remember is that we cannot possibly know all the decisions necessary to fully realize that world as we begin. No matter what name we give to that style, no matter whether we set it in fifteenth century Spain or on a twenty-second century distant planet, whether we limit our world to a Brooklyn kitchen or a South Pacific island, no matter what model we have in mind as our inspiration in the beginning, we can only *project* harmonies. In the beginning, we cannot know what will be in harmony as we finish.

A production's style evolves: choice by choice, action by action, prop by prop, moment by moment. We make an early decision as we choose *this* actor over *that* actor to play the lead. We anticipate following and using certain conventions as we confer with designers. As we rehearse we put some action on stage, some off. We encourage some dialects and discourage others. "Do you want water in the glasses?" a prop person will ask. "How much food is to be eaten?" "How much blood is to be seen?" Again and again we must answer key questions: What is acceptable for that moment? What will seem believable? What will the audience remember?

The theatre is an art form where we must find ways to shape the work, choosing, developing, creating convention after convention to evoke changes in time and place, to evoke parts of characters' lives not seen but only suggested. (No, there is no voice on the other end of that phone conversation, no rain outside the window.) In such a created world we make decision after decision, aiming always toward a believable, significant experience where the audience can bring its memories without stopping to question our choices.

It's easy to forget how many careful decisions must be made as we evolve the conventions necessary to suggest—to evoke— all the time, all the places, all the energy, all the emotional intensity necessary for the believable, significant re-creation of the best of our universal experiences.

Style—what to include, what to leave out? What shape and intensity, what mindsets, what ways of seeing? How can we evolve a style that not only doesn't get in the way of the connection between the audience and the world of the play, but enhances that connection? That delights them? That delights audience and performer?

Evolving the style of a production: It's a job—a serious, time-consuming job. Like the best of poetry, it takes time to distill theatre effort and see what belongs. To be creative is not enough. By definition, avant-garde is creative. But too often theatre strives to be unique for its own sake. We forget we must start with the story's dramatic core. We become enamored with staged metaphor. We put together intellectual ideas of experience, not re-creations of experience. We produce styles that are clever, but do not plunge deep, that do not take us there. We produce illustrated lectures—productions that, clever as they may be, transport neither audience nor actors to that time and place where the experience is bone deep. The action does not grow out of these characters.

On the other hand, a scene can be believable, but not significant enough to justify what is going to happen at the end of the play. An actor can be believable, but doesn't give another actor enough cause to propel her to become the instigator of the plot at the beginning of the next scene. An actor can be believable, but it just doesn't seem important enough to those of us in the audience that we come to root for her—to care whether she is able to emerge the winner or not. Quality theatre—it must be believable *and* significant. Every time.

Theatre, at its best, is an incredibly personal art form. I believe we can seldom create quality theatre if the story we are trying to tell isn't about us. Somehow, we must find a way to enter into that story, that unique and yet universal experience, and we must be determined to bring it to life again and again. Determined to bring it to life piece by piece in rehearsal, determined to distill those discoveries into a harmonious whole for our first audiences, and determined to sustain that oneness where every piece belongs despite the influences of people and events over which we often have very little control. For, unlike a painting or a film, a theatre production in performance is alive—subject to the influences of daily life. At its worst, it reflects our inevitable distractions: a family illness, financial challenges, lost or changed relationships. At its best, it incorporates the richness from experiences that bring us new layers of understanding.

Style—for a theatre production—is not a one-time challenge. What seemed like a perfect harmony of elements yesterday can become a mishmash tomorrow. We only have to remember our disappointment when seeing a tired performance by a road company or when attending a production in a half-empty house as it nears the end of a too-long run.

In style, as in everything else about the theatre, the human being is at the center. And the human being, as we've repeatedly noted, is incredibly complex. We give names to behaviors and tendencies suggesting we know their causes or their functions, suggesting we have a common understanding of their subtleties. But what, for example, do we mean by *realistic acting*? Nothing that contributes to the style of a production is more elusive than descriptions of an actor's style. It is easy to understand and share our choices when we speak of simple physical elements: "In *this* production," for example, "how many actors do we need to make a crowd?" But that tells us nothing about what the people in our crowd will do, how each of them will behave—in short, what their *style* of acting will be on this stage, what will make it one with the rest of the play, what will be in harmony with the world we've created, what about the crowd will make the play happen.

For the best of scenes there will be an almost infinite number of choices that must come together to make the perfect style—the harmony of choices that makes the scene believable and significant.

Here's a simplified breakdown of an actor's work: At any given time, one can identify three tracks he is developing. One is the spoken track—the words he must say. A second is what he does—where he walks or sits, how he uses his cup or sword. A third track carries the emotional state of the character—when does he first begin to rebel? How angry does he become? How angry must he become *now* in order for us to believe he will return to this moment as he confronts the neighbor at the door in the second act?

In working with actors, it was often clear to me they were struggling when trying to make these three tracks work together in time—struggling to keep them synchronized. They might use up all their planned physical action before the long speech was finished. They might clearly exhaust their anger, but still have more words the playwright had given them to be said. They might invent a complex piece of business, but the rhythm of the words to be spoken and that action didn't match. The speech was over but they were still on the wrong side of the room. In short, the style of the words, the actions, and the feelings were not a whole. They didn't track together. Not in this scene. Not for this actor. Not for this play.

This three-track model for analysis is fairly obvious, but the task becomes far more complex when we recognize how the reactions of other actors in the scene can alter what is appropriate for any of these three tracks. The first seeds of disharmony are not always apparent, but soon we all recognize the result. We've seen it many times.

It may seem logical to set *Julius Caesar* in Chicago in the twenties. Intellectually, we can justify the new environment. We see the possibilities for the play's core being made more immediate in this new world. But when you are faced with the challenging demands of a consistent style for all of the scenes— every essential moment of the play—it may or may not be possible to bring all the elements into a unified, harmonious whole. And even if you do, will the company be able to find that harmony next month or in three months, after absorbing the comments and reactions of critics and audiences—after the small but too often significant "improvements" one or another of their fellow actors decides to incorporate in their performance?

One of the reasons I can become absorbed in the evolution of a high-quality basketball team is that their challenge parallels the challenge confronting a production company. To play their best, as individuals and as a team, requires that all those subtle, small choices—those decisions made so quickly one wonders how the possibilities are even seen, let alone realized— requires that all of those choices come together again and again in near perfect harmony.

Moreover, the degree of alertness, the degree of sensitivity, the amount of energy demanded for the best performances is determined not only by the work of individuals and their interaction with fellow players, but also from the reaction of the spectators. In our sports-addicted nation, we know all about this. Sports writers refer to it in every day's newspapers. Most of us have felt it. The audience can be electrified by the tension as a close game against a strong opponent moves to its finish. Afterward, we say, "It was unforgettable!" We recognized it for what it was: their best effort against enormous challenges. We saw them working together in amazing ways, unique ways during each performance, ways incredibly difficult to repeat. And they counted on us. Their energy depended on our energy. They performed better because we were there. No one doubts it. The very best athletic teams will do it again and again. And so will the actors in the great productions.

But not without an enormous amount of preparation and a clear understanding of the task ahead. Not without an absolute certainty of the essentials at the core of their work. And—even then—the final result will not always be enough. Not today. Not this time. Human beings forget. Automatic pilots take over. Old habits reemerge. We are distracted at the crucial time.

Next time.... We'll have to start differently. We'll have to be more careful. More free. A slightly different mindset. More invested in....

True for the best of athletic teams. True for the best of theatre companies.

I am reminded of my own company's efforts to re-create key historical events in the lives of Lincoln and other Americans. As we sought to renew the actors' investment in scenes from the Civil War, for example, events that carried considerable emotional power for the performers as a result of our work during rehearsals, we often found it necessary to give those historic accounts renewed meaning during the long run by looking for parallel stories. A long run does that: It lessens the impact of the key moments in the story if there is no effort to find new ways of suggesting the universal recurrence of such moments. Any actor challenged to repeat a story again and again for the living theatre audience will need to recognize the power of parallel experiences. The long run makes acting for the theatre very different from acting for film or television. Each performance will be unique, just as each original experience is unique, but all will also have much in common with other experiences of that action. To look for fresh, revitalizing models from the day's news, from stories of other times and places, deepens the understanding and emotional texture of the original story's performance. Unique and yet repeated again and again. Universal and yet never twice exactly the same.

I came to appreciate how much a production inevitably changes, how it evolves even after it opens, after it has run for fifty or a hundred performances.

Our play about Lincoln and the Civil War changed again and again over seventeen seasons—often subtle changes, sometimes only for a performance or two, but changes nevertheless. Changes that enriched and changes that distracted. I remember how one summer none of us could escape the impact of a solitary figure standing in Tiananmen Square, his defiance stopping the rumbling tanks sent to quell student protest. Somehow, our historical play about Lincoln and America was also about China and the struggles in Beijing that season—more than a hundred years after the events we were depicting. Here was a production whose style had been fixed and polished from initial preparation through performance after performance, recast and re-rehearsed again and again, performed through multiple seasons, and yet this singular, distant event lent a new and different texture to more than one moment in the complex shaping of our offering.

Granted, the three plays in our trilogy were dense—hundreds of characters and many, many events—but some of the most interesting audience reactions often came from people who saw the same scripts produced over many performances and many seasons. I would hear, "You've added some things, haven't you?" "You've changed the script." I almost never had, of course. And, while we constantly worked to bring more life to certain scenes, while the style of the productions remained essentially the same, there were obviously differences. Some of that can be accounted for by recognizing that the audiences brought their own changes—changes in interests and insights— but this living theatre that sought to tell essentially the same stories again and again was never quite twice the same.

The director's challenge is to keep those changes adding to, not distracting from, the believability and significance of the dramatic action at the play's core. That action must happen and we must care—care deeply—no matter what the inevitable changes. No matter how the production's style continues to evolve.

Out of such contradictions came a wonderfully useful model for my own thinking about the act of creating. We had just completed a powerful exploration and set of performances of *Quilters*, the play based on interviews of women descended from pioneers in the early American Southwest. Playing to sold-out houses, its viewers included multiple generations of rural Midwestern women—grandmothers and mothers and their children—who sat riveted by the accounts of lives paralleling the stories they had heard from their own ancestors. As I watched, it occurred to me what a wonderful metaphor the quilt was for the evolution of a production's style: We borrow from the pieces and tatters of those who have gone before, from their viewpoints and their creations, and we piece together a new work, enormously dependent on those patterns from the past. What emerges has a new style, unique and yet far from unique, containing at once tatters from worker after worker whose lives are represented in the pieces we use to create, and containing our own stitching, holding together this current piece—this story in its new form with its new harmonies, told here for these people—*now*.

I have seen few "original" quilts—quilts made from worn tatters of material tied to the lives of the families of the creators—that weren't things of beauty. That weren't art of significance. And in the living theatre, in a sense, all performances have the potential to be an original quilt created from pieces of the past. How the work is put together, how carefully it is stitched—its final pattern, its pattern *tonight*—is the style, the unique style for this story's re-creation as it is shared by these people with this audience. Like the finest of quilts, the very best in the theatre will bring all those tattered pieces from our lives together into a single whole where everything belongs. Will bring it together *tonight*.

And tomorrow—with a different audience in what may or may not feel like a very different time—we will try again. Try again for the perfect harmony.

No, you may not have the designers who worked on the New York production. Your lead may not be the equal of the actor who starred in the film. But use your best resources to their full advantage, fit them together, oh, so carefully, and who knows? You may suddenly find you have an unforgettable experience.

Last summer, I watched my two-and-a-half-year-old granddaughter pull on her dress-up clothes, arrange her tiny doll furniture in a circle around her in the living room, and with great deliberation and dignity set about the serious business of feeding her family—two dolls, a stuffed mouse, and a dragon. She made a lot of choices. And watching her care for her children was delightful. I can say with confidence that every choice she made was her own. It needed to be done. The pieces fit. Even the crown she wore—the one with the plastic would-be diamonds—seemed perfect. It was clearly her style at work. Her very personal, two-and-a-half-year-old viewpoint.

Utter harmony.

Would that more theatre could do as much.

#5: Build an ensemble that grows through sharing story after story. FOSTER THEIR BELIEF IN THEATRE AS A COMMUNAL EXPERIENCE WHERE THE AUDIENCE IS A VALUED CONTRIBUTOR.

There is a simple but basic truth we sometimes lose sight of: Even the more successful actors who make a living working in the American theatre are out of a job much of the time.

For most, it means they are constantly preparing to audition. It means *looking* for work. Doing other things to keep

73

busy—and to earn a living. For many, if they're lucky, it means making commercials so the residuals will pay the rent or the mortgage. How much practice of their craft do actors get? How much opportunity to rehearse, act in quality scripts, play challenging characters that offer opportunites to learn? For most—even the more successful ones—not much. Growth in such a system is in fits and starts, serious regressions and— maybe—occasionally, significant learnings.

Here's a thought: In the ideal world, the world that would be most satisfying and most productive, actors would *live* someplace. And they would *work* there. Work as *actors*. No, not go to New York or to Los Angeles to be discovered—they would actually become part of something. By choice. Become part of a community. Put down roots. Be in a place they care about. Get a life. Live someplace where being there makes a difference.

And not just actors. Isn't the same true for playwrights and directors? For designers and stage managers? For costumers and prop masters? What would happen if success didn't mean they would get a chance to go somewhere *else*? Successful in New York so they can live in Fuji. Successful in LA so they can live in Paris. Successful in Chicago so they can live in London. What if success meant you could just stay home? Stay home and love it.

Home.

This chapter is about creating a home for the theatre and for the people who work in the theater. A place where real growth can happen. A place with possibilities only dimly suggested by those early classes and first lucky breaks. There are a few homes for the theatre in America—a few, but not many. For twenty years I had one of those homes.   Like many, I had always assumed it would be easy to bring together a group of talented theatre people I knew with whom it would be a delight to create theatre—should that opportunity ever arise. In the middle of our first season I realized we knew a great deal about preparing a production, but we knew almost nothing about sustaining a company. Challenged by financial shortfalls and serious conflict among personnel, those first years quickly made anything more than bare-bones survival seem an almost utopian goal. And yet—somehow—as time passed, the gift of having our own theatre company in what was, in many respects, an ideal location for it began to trump our struggles. I began to understand the real interconnectedness of the ensemble, the audience, and the material. I had no desire to be someplace else. No desire to have my theatre in New York or Los Angeles.

It became the most powerful learning experience of my professional life.

Our first four chapters have dealt with changes we might make in working on a production—a single production. This fifth possibility suggests a more far-reaching change in direction; it challenges us to consider the potential learning that a team can do versus the learning that is possible when we work as individuals. It asks us to examine these four issues:

- The potential interdependence of a community and a resident theatre.
- The challenges to sustaining a quality ensemble.
- The fundamental roles in a creative theatre ensemble.
- The growth only a sustained ensemble can produce.

Maybe it isn't enough to do theatre because we enjoy doing theatre. Maybe it isn't enough to find a script now and then that speaks to us, one we feel should be seen. Maybe it isn't enough to do Shakespeare because we all know Shakespeare was a great playwright, to bring the classics or the Best of Broadway to the hinterlands—or to Boston or Memphis or San Diego, for that matter. Maybe it isn't even enough to give new playwrights a chance to be seen in Pasadena or Colorado Springs.

To do *great* theatre, don't we have to explore the bone deep concerns of a community—the experiences that count most? Isn't that what the Greeks did? And Elizabethan England? Isn't that what the Federal Theatre Project was attempting to do during the Great Depression? What about the theatre of Eastern Europe when they were trying to fight back against the occupation of the Soviets? What about the Russian theatre itself when it was trying to make the Soviet system work after overthrowing the tsar?

When I taught my first theatre classes, nearly fifty years ago, I used to read aloud passages from an essay by playwright Robert Sherwood. First published in *Theatre Arts Magazine* some twenty years before that, it was titled "The Dwelling Place of Wonder" and it began, "When I contemplate the present state of the theatre I am deeply moved to ask myself, 'Why am I in it?'" It was a long reading, full of references to Hamlet and Oedipus and Prometheus, with stirring passages that must have been an unexpected beginning for the new theatre student, even then. Things like this: "The dramatist cannot be dismissed as merely a successful merchant of wish fulfillment. For there is historical proof that every age which has produced great dramatists—in Greece, in England and Germany and France— has presaged an age of renewed, vigorous assertion of human rights."

As he neared the end of this essay, written only a few months before the December 7, 1941 attack on Pearl Harbor, Sherwood prophetically wrote, "[The American dramatist] does not have to look into legend to find assurance of the essential heroism and nobility of man; he has only to look into this morning's newspaper."

"…into this morning's newspaper."

When it comes to creating a theatre that counts, it's all there—all there in the voices around us.

Life is not bland. Put twenty people in a room and my experience tells me there will be at least one unknown story among them that, if told well, would knock your socks off. That's the first reward for a strong connection between the theatre and its community: If you can tap it, there will be an astounding reservoir of dramatic, untold, potentially powerful stories all around you. The need is not for better material, the need is to connect with it. To learn how to mine that material and to develop the tools to bring it to life.

It is no accident that some of America's greatest music came from slaves, that all of us celebrate what came to be known as "the Birth of the Blues." Consider our great writers and our great photographers who sought to give voice to the Great Depression, to World War II, and to the Vietnam War. To give voice to the aging, to women's demand for the vote and equal pay. Consider those who sought to give a face to Appalachia, to the dust bowl, to the inner city, to the immigrant, to the builders and explorers, to the desperate and the determined.

The theatre will be great again only when it speaks for a great cause. Only when it is connected to something larger than itself.

Yes, I know about the classics. I understand that, for the past fifty or more years, the surest road to sustaining a theatre company in America seems to have been the Shakespeare festival. But could the assumption that Shakespeare is the surest way to find an audience be one of the contributors to our mediocrity in the theatre? I started my own theatre focused on Lincoln and American history because I refused to believe the only great writer worth building an American theatre around was one who had lived in another country and had been dead for almost four hundred years. And even if you love "the classics"—and we won't all agree on that list, will we?—I have found that when I know the community, know why I am trying to give voice to that community's concerns, to offer even a familiar classic to that community can significantly change the experience of the play.

Have you ever served on a play selection committee for an organization that didn't know why it was producing plays? A company that couldn't find a script they wanted to explore? When it comes to identifying goals and mission, a theatre company should have an important advantage over almost every other company I can think of: The basics of theatre all have to do with human relationships. We don't have to go to the Amazon to find the essential raw materials. We don't have to develop sophisticated new technology requiring months or years of research and hundreds of thousands or millions of dollars invested in laboratories and equipment. We don't have to find new sources of power, new forms of transportation, new means of distribution, new media for mass marketing. We only need to bring together a group of highly motivated, creative people. Bring them together in a place where they can listen to the voices surrounding them and take the memory of *that* into a safe, quiet world where they—together, together as play-*wrights*—heat that memory and bend it and distill it until a drama emerges worthy of the voices from which it began. And then give them—give that ensemble—the opportunity to share their creation with audiences that have the potential to be significantly impacted by the offering—let them share it again and again. And if that can happen, *as* that happens, have that ensemble develop ways to learn from the reaction of their audiences and with their new learnings—from the audiences, from working with the material, and from each other—ask them to start again. Start again, building on the learnings from this time and the time before and the time before that.

It sounds simple.

It isn't.

To create high quality theatre an ensemble needs to become experienced and wise in understanding the way each individual works with the others, in understanding the world they seek to re-create, and in understanding those with whom they would share. It needs to evolve a system for learning how to be artists in an art form that requires we create *together*.

We are after a high-performance team, not just a collection of people brought together to put on a play. No, not even a collection of successful, skilled and talented artists will do, if they have little understanding of the learning system they need to evolve.

I remember how startled I was when, many years ago, a student in one of my rehearsal classes said, "I feel like we come to church when we come in here." My first image was of passion plays and the few religious dramas I had seen—far from what I thought were my own best models. And yet, as Sherwood wrote in that same *Theatre Arts* essay, "...what the theatre has been for, from its very beginning—[is] to make credible the incredible, to awaken the king that dwells in every humble man, the hero in every coward." I believed then, as I do now, in what Sherwood sought to remind us: "A great play...is a great inspiration, and its performance is a kind of revivalist meeting. The great dramatist is one who knows that in the tragedy of blindness Oedipus discovered the inward power to see the ultimate truth."

Building an ensemble that seeks to grow through sharing story after story implicitly starts by accepting the challenge to better understand human relationships. Consciously or unconsciously that will be the agreement—spoken or unspoken.

And is that what we have been trained for? Is that the core of the performer's training? Probably not. And yet...is the theatre exempt from the questioning facing nearly every system where we live, work, struggle, raise our children—where we seek, share, earn, give and receive as we go about our daily pursuits in the America of the twenty-first century?

Consider the long-established Broadway hierarchy with its star-driven long runs. Consider the continual forming and re-forming of companies to produce a single script in the hope it will be a hit. Consider a star system where an actor whose reputation was built on internationally successful films, but who often has little or no experience on stage, is often the anchor of a company whose success or failure will be measured by how many people see the production.

I hear no one in the theatre wondering why it has become standard practice for the artistic directors of our most respected theatres to spend more of their time directing for other companies than for their own. Who tends the store while they are away? Who is responsible for sustaining the quality of the work? Who is studying the links between the community and the theatre to develop the next set of projects? Is that what we need from leadership if we are to have a great theatre? One worth rescuing against the odds?

Maybe if we want higher quality theatre, we really don't have to weigh the advantages of promoting individual careers versus developing high quality production companies—maybe we already know the answer to that choice. If the NBA and NFL understand it takes more than one star to create a winning team, if athletic coaches in a sports-obsessed nation understand the power of team building, surely the theatre has the possibility of tapping into that insight. Maybe we just have to learn *how* to make our theatre companies healthy, make them nurturing environments, places that feed the souls of all those who work there, make them more productive when measured by our best values, make them more responsive to their communities and more highly prized by those communities.

One of my own most valued theatre practices began out of desperation. We had had a great opening week. Wonderful audiences. Excellent reviews. And then the weather turned questionable. For an outdoor theatre—as I soon learned—this was a potential disaster. Our attendance dropped dramatically. As the actors' morale nosedived, I decided to try to get them in touch with the enthusiasm of those viewers who did appear, those who had traveled long distances, determined to find out what we had to offer.

It was a simple beginning, but one of the most highly productive practices of my directing career: We began to have the actors greet the audience as they arrived, to move among them and find out who they were and why they came. We bounded down off the stage following the curtain call and lined up at the exits to talk with them as they left.

We learned all kinds of things from those audiences: about their families, about their travels, about American history, about Lincoln and his connection to their personal histories. We discovered we were all part of the same community and that we had all been drawn here by Lincoln and the American experience. (Sound familiar?) About half of them came from within two hundred miles; the other half came from all over the world. It was an education. And we used it. We used it as we developed new works. We used it to try to keep the current works alive. We borrowed their energy. We had them write out their responses and we reported those to our granting organizations.

We saw five generations from one family in the theatre one night and we talked about that. We had local folk in the audience who counted their return visits. We were invited into their homes and to their church picnics. We had volunteers who ushered and took tickets and we listened to their stories and wove the tales of their ancestors into our accounts of more widely known American pioneers. We celebrated the 4th of July on their lakes with them, and at our own special performances we gave out candles and lit them together as we sang our finale. We brought in descendants of the figures in the plays who sat around bonfires and talked into the nights with us.

It was a homecoming.

"Shouldn't we be in New York?" some asked. "Shouldn't we be in Chicago?" "What about Washington?" Surely there was someone who would want us in Washington. And occasionally we did travel—a performance here, a performance there. But we knew: Our roots were here in the cornfields. Here, where Lincoln and his friends, his opponents, his descendants, and his followers, his well-intended and not so well-intended followers, had lived. Here under the star-strewn sky when the last stage lights went out.

I used to describe our company as a repository for the experiences that had built America. I'm not sure I would ever have thought to do that had the grant writing for the Illinois Humanities Council not seemed to demand it—to find a justification beyond the usual arts assumptions. And yet, now, in retrospect, it seems to have been an important description. We *were* a living library. A modest one to be sure. Not a huge number of volumes. Not an enormous edifice to house our collection. But we had a lot of threads running through those works. A lot of connections. And it was pretty clear: those connections would have been very difficult to maintain had we somehow moved to New York.

We all know we need an audience to complete the theatre event: an actor and an audience—the two essentials. But most of the time, it seems to me, we evaluate our audiences by a bottom-line business mentality: How many people see our shows and how much income does it produce? I suppose some would say there is a corollary: Who supports our work and how much money are they willing to contribute?

It will come as no surprise that I believe the sad state of the current theatre is due in no small measure to our willingness to evaluate the theatre's success almost entirely by those questions. *Survival* may be measured by those questions, but *success*, as my long-time colleague and dear friend Roman Tymchyshyn used to say, "...is another pair of galoshes."

The point here is not that we can ignore fiscal reality, but that, if we are to produce theatre of significantly higher quality, we must give a great deal more attention to developing insight and practices for high-performance creative teams. We must consciously focus on leadership for those teams, on attracting and developing unique contributors, on tools for sustaining those teams, and on insuring they are intrinsically bound to their communities and to the human concerns that shape the values of performers and audiences alike. It is not a study that, it seems to me, has been given our best effort.

In short, the kind of creative ensembles we are able to develop and nurture will likely have more long-term effect on the quality of the American theatre than any single production in our current, Broadway oriented, long-run system no matter how celebrated that production or how extended its tours to the "wastelands."

The people you select in the beginning are really important; try to hold on to the ones who get it. But the ones you add—and if you can sustain the effort there will be many—are equally important. Important, because, as you grow, you will begin to better understand what you are missing, what you need. It is essential to have healthy leadership from a number of people in any ensemble; most of those leaders will probably develop their understanding through maturation, working within the system—*if* it is a system with an end the best of them respect and are fed by. Given the climate of America's professional theatre, be alert for those who model respect for this work instead of forever seeking greater material awards. Be alert for people who have already tested the water, who know what it is to work in other systems—systems that more naïve ensemble members may tend to envy for their popular status. Currently, most theatre people think, "If I can only get to the next level I will have arrived." Those levels are all too often less than satisfying.

It's inevitable that some won't fit, however great their skills. After a season or a production they may need to move on to some other effort. No matter how skilled they are, if they're not able to work within the company's system as really significant contributors, it's good to wish them well and let them go. One of the most valuable evolutions for any company, any ensemble, is a process for such separations. A process that feels fair and honest for all and one that allows—in fact, encourages—the separation without leaving behind rancor and hostility. Remember, it's possible that a reunion under different circumstances at a different time may make that person's rejoining the ensemble a gift for all. Try to make every departure one where that could be welcomed.

Seek to create a theatre that says, of all the places I could work, for me, this is the best—best for my professional growth, best for my enjoyment of the community, best because I'm needed and valued. It's a place where I can feel I'm an artist whose insight has the potential to be nurtured with every project. It's a place where I'm willing to give my strongest effort and invest sustained energy without reservation. It deserves my commitment.

Creative theatre minds could do worse than undertake a serious exploration of the readily available material about *systems*, about *leadership and the organization*, and about the development of *high-performance teams*. As a starter, I can imagine few who wouldn't profit from a look at Margaret Wheatley's writings—the ground-breaking *Leadership and the New Science* may be off-putting to some, but *A Simpler Way*, co-authored with Myron Kellner-Rogers, has a format likely to be inviting to any who find the improvisations and impulses of the creative arts a long way from most five-year plans and bottom lines. Its words often seem more poetry than prose: "Human organizations are not the lifeless machines we wanted them to be," they write.

It may be reassuring to you, as it was to me, to read their assertion: "Systems can't be known ahead of time. Until the system forms, we have very limited knowledge of what might emerge. The only way to know a system is to play with it. Life's restless urge to experiment and discover, its great tinkering, its wild surprises, invite us to become experimenters...."

"Tinkering." Most theatre people should be comfortable with that. In the real world, some of our most important insights come from tinkering to meet a small problem, only to discover the change takes us to a long-needed new practice. There is more wisdom in *A Simpler Way*, of course. For me, little is more important than this: "Identity is the source of organization. Every organization is an identity in motion, moving through the world, trying to make a difference. Therefore the most important work we can do at the beginning of an organizing effort is to engage one another in exploring our purpose."

People coming together for any purpose bring a collection of diverse life experiences: baggage—good and bad. Any ensemble is challenged again and again to find ways to overcome suspicion and envy, insecurity and self-interest. The best ensembles—the most productive—are collections of trusting partners united by a common value. It's a bit daunting to realize that any group of twenty includes 190 potential one-to-one relationships. Some will quickly become nurturing partnerships, some will be tolerant but isolated individuals, and a few will band together to encourage one another at the expense of still others.

The child in each of us *will* reappear. At best, that child will be a marvelous source of insight and sensitivity. At worst, that child can create conflict that not only interrupts creative progress, but severely damages the company's confidence that this is a safe and nurturing place to be.

In any ensemble, one-to-one partnerships will be formed to help counteract insecurity and bring insight, but they can also feed the perception of slights both real and imagined. They can feed envy and destructive judgments. To develop a highly creative, trusting team—a nurturing ensemble—means we must be vigilant in developing ways to resolve the inevitable conflicts and in weeding out those familiar, destructive partnerships of encouragement that scapegoat others.

And just what did Robert Sherwood mean when he titled his *Theatre Arts* article "The Dwelling Place of Wonder"? Was he urging us to recapture our childhood sense of awe? Well, perhaps. But it was more than that. "The theatre is the spiritual home," he wrote, "of one who is barred from the church by distaste for dogma but who still requires and demands expression of great faith." And wherever we stand in regard to church or dogma, isn't that last inevitably true: the best theatre will be an "expression of great faith"? It will give voice to the soul. Why? Because it will again and again tap our most vulnerable selves, demand we interact in ways that expose our most intimate thoughts, and expose and prod us to reexamine our most soulful yearnings.

So the challenge is considerable, this business of creating an ensemble that stays together—that is willing to stay together, no, *eager* to stay together—and that grows from doing play after play in order to learn to tap their potentially highest values, their expression of great faith. The challenge is considerable for the ensemble to be creating out of trust of one another and a genuine recognition that as each member of the ensemble grows it helps the others learn. We have the possibility of becoming great artists as we are surrounded by other quality artists—

artists whose work inspires us with their modeling and their desire to see us succeed.

The most fruitful strategies for creating such a team are complex and difficult to prescribe generically. Each effort will demand unique solutions. Hints, models—possibilities can be gathered from an enormous variety of sources. Given the opportunity, each of us will have had experiences suggesting useful starting places. Tinkering—that's the demand. Continual tinkering spurred on by an agreed-upon purpose that reflects the community in which we choose to live, tinkering that helps us voice the values and concerns of that community.

A few words about the makeup of the ensemble itself: Most of the time when we speak of a theatre ensemble, we think of a group of actors—actors who work well together respecting the contribution of each without undue attention given to the stars. Before leaving the ideal of a high-performance team for the theatre, let me suggest an expansion of that definition:

Long ago, Max Reinhardt said that everyone who works in the theatre should be an actor. He meant that metaphorically, of course, but there is something to be said for taking that literally. What if everyone who contributed to a production was at some time capable of playing roles—even small ones—in the productions of that company? I happen to believe we have lost something very important by our emphasis on specialization in the theatre. There is a great deal to be said for learning firsthand how a production and an audience interact and how the members of an ensemble interact with one another—in both rehearsal *and* performance. In short, I question whether we can produce our best theatre without our playwrights, our directors, and our designers having a more sustained connection with the process. All too often a number of key contributors to the productions I've been around seldom see the production's evolution in rehearsal. They seldom appreciate the difficulties of maintaining that production's quality during the long run or the effect of differing audience reactions on a given night's performance. Sometimes key contributors never even see the full production in performance. For me, this suggests we should be far more open to nurturing young, would-be artists from among the ensemble's actors to play one of these other principal roles in varying productions. Why not? Why not have plays in repertory where the director of one production plays a small role in another? Why not have plays in repertory where one script is written by an actor who acts in still another, wearing a costume designed by the lead in a third?

My own experiences in the theatre eventually came to focus on directing. But in those few later career instances where I chose to act, I was reminded of important challenges I had ceased to give full credit when I was not the one in the trenches. Those observations became available because I was one of the cast, preparing and acting day after day. I saw them in my own needs and distractions and I saw them in others. For a director who tried to be sensitive to the actor's experience in both rehearsal and performance, it was a sobering realization and an important learning experience.

We develop so many of our most important beliefs through practical experience. Always. Until those experiences are available to us, how can we know what we have yet to learn? For example, a company performing plays in repertory opens up almost unlimited creative possibilities. Yet, so few American actors have had a chance to experience even the most obvious of those benefits: the enrichment of roles that comes from taking on allied but differing tasks on successive nights. In my experience, an actor who plays a lead one night and a small, supporting role the next, or even two very different roles on succeeding nights, has a possibility for growth rarely seen in the single-production long run.

Yes, I know. There are practical issues here. Just as with questions of marketing and developing financial support, practical production practices immediately bring to mind questions of budgets, pay schedules, and working conditions. But the general concept is still worth examining: How can we best insure that the creative work—*all* the creative work—is by people who have a deep understanding and a strong commitment to the core values of the company *and* the community to which that company belongs?

In retirement, my wife and I travel a great deal. It's been surprising how many cities and towns in America we have seen where they have somehow managed to raise enough funds to erect their own performing arts centers. There is something touchingly poignant in those brick buildings standing in the middle of America's communities. They speak of a yearning for others to know. For a people's voice to be heard.

Too often we see those buildings standing empty as they await the Broadway shows coming in November or April, shows that are coming to bring the "Best of Broadway" to Kansas and Kentucky. In this diverse America that likes to think of itself as a beacon for people's struggles for democracy everywhere, isn't there something telling about our building such edifices only to have them sit waiting for distant artists to fill them?

"Yes," you might say, "but how many *Waiting for Guffmans* do we need?" Perhaps. But there is also that other possibility: the possibility that if they keep at it long enough, if they nurture one another enough, if they work hard enough at finding out who they are and what life has told them, there just might be a Chekhov or Brecht among them and a really gifted actor or two. There may even be a really sensitive director who emerges. And if none emerges, but the "home" that's being built can become attractive enough, isn't it possible some of those partially employed theatre people waiting tables in LA or New York might just prefer to set down roots here *if* the community makes clear it wants creative people who can give them a voice as badly as they wanted a building for the appearance of an occasional road company?

Early in my career as a university faculty member, I was very aware how many of us believed the "professional" theatre was where the "real" theatre experience was offered. Today, I am struck by the number of "professionals" I know who have left New York or Los Angeles to work on a college campus

because that "real" career too often left them unsatisfied, sometimes bitter, and almost always exhausted.

There are huge numbers of trained theatre people in
America; there are thousands of people with BA and BFA and
even MFA and PhD degrees in some facet of theatre. There are
hundreds of thousands of others who have acted or designed
or worked backstage and found it fed something important to
them personally. Today, only a small percentage of them continue to try to be a part of the living theatre.

Maybe we've made a simple but serious mistake: Maybe
we've assumed we know what the theatre can be and we just
need the money to do it and the audience to support it. If
we want the living theatre to survive, if we want it to fill a
few more of those performing arts centers scattered over the
American landscape with real quality, maybe we have to refo-
cus our efforts. Maybe we need to find ways to attract people
who want to be *here*, to put down roots *here*, to learn the possibilities for bringing alive the stories of the struggles and hopes
of the people *here*. Maybe we need to choose our classics more
carefully when we want to go outside for a script, choose plays
because they seem to offer something special for concerns that
surround us *here*, surround us *now*. Maybe we need more than
playwriting contests and artist grants—maybe we need connections. Real connections. Maybe we need a more deeply rooted
interest in one another.

And if we should have some success, if, by some chance, we
should find a significant audience and significant financial support, maybe we will be lucky and not become enamored with
growing too large—so large our creative ensemble, our high-
performance team, stops being a team. Maybe our best people
will think twice before running off to New York or Los Angeles
if someone dangles a contract. And maybe we'll resist building
too elaborate a building, too huge a monument with too many
nameplates of contributors and too much marble. Maybe we'll
recognize it for what it's becoming: a dwelling place of wonder.

And that will be enough. Even if it's for only a little while, that will be enough.

David Abram, in *The Spell of the Sensuous,* wrote, "The telling of stories, like singing and praying, would seem to be an almost ceremonial act, an ancient and necessary mode of speech that tends the earthly rootedness of human language. For narrated events...always happen *somewhere.* And for an oral culture, that locus is never merely incidental to those occurrences. The events belong...to the place, and to tell the story of those events is to let the place itself, speak through the telling."

Maybe, if a few of those companies can create piece after piece that lives up to the theatre's potential, the communities they've given voice won't let their theatres die. Maybe if the work is good enough, they'll be treasured—at least for a little while. And everyone who is part of that happening will know he or she has done something. In an America hungry for tools that help us really connect, maybe they'll know they've done something.

#6: Use pretty pictures with caution. SEE THAT DESIGNS, NO MATTER HOW INVENTIVE, DO NOT REPLACE BELIEVABLE, SIGNIFICANT HUMAN EXPERIENCE AS THE PRODUCTION'S CORE.

We have a product misrepresentation that's widespread in America. It's called *packaging*. At the supermarket it's often plastic, and much of it ends up in our landfills. Environmentalists have been railing against it for some time now, but there it is: enormous dumpsters and burial grounds full of it. At first it's attractive in the ads, eye-catching on the shelves. So, we bring it home. And, if you're like me, more than once you've begun to swear just at the difficulty of getting it open. The difficulty of finding the thing you paid for somewhere inside—past the cardboard and plastic and Styrofoam.

I won't extend this metaphor any longer—you get the idea. And, of course, not all packaging is bad. It would be difficult to take home a pound of ground coffee in our hands. And I, personally, am still tempted to chuck my old cell phone just to get a new iPhone for the simple reason that I love the look of the thing. But here's my point: I believe the American theatre is much better at packaging than creating content. So much so, that we have produced very talented, creative designers whose settings, costumes, props, lighting effects, projections, and goodness knows what else have become the central value and core standard for all too many of our offerings. In the theatre, we are—more often than not—selling the wrappers. Glitz reigns.

"And why shouldn't we?" you say. Isn't that the *American way*? Well, yes, I guess it is. We do have an enormous number of products on the shelves, after all, and many of them are almost the same, so how else does one stand out? But I believe the theatre has the potential to be an extremely rewarding product, and too often there's very little of it in the package.

Don't get me wrong, I think good design can make a tremendous difference in the theatre: good design that supports the dramatic action of the play. Good design that helps the actors tell the story, helps define the characters, helps raise the stakes.

But beware of designs that leave the audience awed by their beauty and cleverness and wondering what the play was about.

Production support tends to be divided into two principal camps in America. In one camp there isn't enough money, shop skill, or sophisticated design sense. Whether it's the high school drama group, the community theatre, or the non-profit professional theatre around the corner, the tech support is often amateurish. Occasionally, the actors are good enough, the director is insightful enough, and the play choice is wise enough that the less than skillful tech work doesn't matter. With better design support the production might be more powerful and memorable, but in these rare cases, the human depictions at its core win out. What the play is trying to say emerges under what many would suspect are the most trying of circumstances. When we find such a production, most of us are filled with wonder. No budget, no real production support—and yet it worked! As Pogo used to say, "Hooraw!"

The other theatre camp has a significant—or at least reasonable—production budget and frequent access to quality designers and shops with skilled craftspeople. Equipment and talent are sufficient to produce impressive lighting and sound with options for original musical underscores and video projections—sometimes properties and makeup to rival Disney World or Hollywood. These productions are usually found on Broadway, at our best-known Shakespeare festivals, at some of our regional resident theatres, and among our better university and college theatre offerings.

Nearly all of them would declare they are handicapped by tight budgets and insufficient time, but make no mistake about it, well-trained, talented, skilled artisans work in this second group of American theatres—people who reflect the insight and taste of a culture where graphic design and advertising art surround us every day, decorating where we sleep, eat, and escape. When it comes to design, they know what they're doing, and this "half" of the American theatre gives them a chance to show their wares. If we are willing to spend the money for admission, we can see some impressive work.

And that's the problem: Too often theatre professionalism is measured by how much money and design expertise are lavished on the production.

I have come to see this as blatant seduction of the most obvious kind. It looks good in the photographs we publish in our flyers and magazines of record. It includes music we play on our iPods. It dazzles us for the first five minutes after the curtain goes up—although for many productions, five minutes of dazzle is probably stretching it.

It reflects our acceptance of the quick fix. It's billboard art. Art for the passerby.

In America, the America of so little time and so many demands for our attention, those who are quality practitioners of quick-fix art can often name their rewards. In short, we know all about their selling of virtual beauty. Long ago we grew accustomed to seeing it when it came to marketing the Hollywood starlet or—in today's version—the next American Idol. We know it so well that when we have a real interest in a product, when we know what we really need, what we really want it to do, we're experienced at looking past the packaging to find the products that deliver. To find the ones with lasting value.

So why is skin-deep beauty so seductive to those who create our theatre? Why are we so ready to spend precious time and money producing it when there is a severely limited engine under the hood? Is it that we are determined to create *something* that tells the audience we know what we're doing, when we either don't know how to give them a better core product or don't think they would recognize such a core product as valuable unless we dress it up in the most expensive, elaborate package we can find? "If it works in *Vanity Fair* or *The New York Times Magazine*, it will work for us!" Is that the theatre's thinking? Is it really that simple?

If it doesn't serve us well, why do we persist? And what *is* the price we pay for all of this?

Let me return to my earlier assertion—the suggestion that when it comes to theatre and design support there are two camps. Here's the simplest answer to that first question, "Why do we persist?" We do it because almost everyone begins work in the theatre as part of the first camp—we know all about the poor theatre where quality technical support is hard to come by. We've been there, done that. We know what it is to work where it would be nice—no, more than nice, it would be incredibly exciting—to have our dreamed-for setting or costumes, but it's seldom possible. In short, we began in a theatre where we *couldn't*, and once we *can*, well, it's hard to resist.

Yes, I know, that's pure speculation on my part, and even if it's true, why would we be willing to do it, if it's detrimental to the whole? So let's take a more considered view.

In really good design for the theatre, the pretty pictures *can't be separated* from the content of the production. By definition, really good design in the theatre is more than pretty pictures. Good design makes it work. The pretty pictures are integral to the play's truthfulness. They raise its significance. They help tell the story. They enrich the core experience. They make a valuable connection by enhancing our understanding of the environment, the characters, and the moment. They help us see the play's passages as universal and significant. Whether it be lighting or costume, set design or stage properties, the experience of the key events of the play are made more moving and more memorable when these support elements are well-designed and well-executed. In the well-designed production, actors are better able to invest in their roles and the cast's experiencing of the action is made more affecting for the audience *because* of support elements that do their job and may or may not be so attractive in themselves. In fact, well-designed elements may or may not be *pretty*, but they *work*.

There's another key standard in play here: quantity. Just as is true of the script and of the actors, in some instances more is better, but just as often, better comes from less. Good design contributes and good design doesn't get in the way. Good design is creative, but is also well edited. It's selective. Very selective. It helps bring together our resources to tell the story. Good design is poetry.

But remember: This is a collaborative art. And how do we know what belongs and what doesn't?

In the timeline of the collective work on a production, there are several key periods where solid agreement and shared vision are necessary but incredibly difficult to come by. It's very easy to have skilled designers of theatre parts who have little understanding of the whole. Some lack understanding because they come from other fields—they are artists or craftspeople who know how to work with clothing or settings but were never really insightful about the core of the theatre. They may be brilliant at designing for shopping malls, store windows, clothing fashions, and a host of other familiar environments and products, but their insight doesn't extend to playwriting, directing, or acting—nothing that close to the human core of the theatre. When they work in the theatre, they rely on others to put their product to good use: "You need a costume for the king—sure, I can give it to you." And they do and it's often beautiful; we don't expect them to write brilliant dialogue or produce believable acting, and when they are good enough at what they do, we are often delighted when we can afford them and we ask little more. Other designers, for whom theatre may be their primary interest through training, experience, or human insight, are much more attuned to the art of the theatre—to the theatre's core—but are often engaged in so many simultaneous, multiple-design projects it becomes nearly impossible for them to have more than a cursory exposure to the day-to-day evolution of the play in rehearsal. And here, let me repeat the obvious: No matter how detailed the early planning, a production evolves through rehearsal in unexpected ways. That is true for the best productions just as much as it is true for the pedestrian productions. (Some might suggest it is more true for the best productions.)

The best designers use time and energy wisely in their own creation, and they help us use time and energy wisely in our work with all the other elements in the production. In a system where rehearsal time is always at a premium, good design can be assimilated into the total effort without shortchanging the actors' experiencing of the play. That's not as obvious as it may sound. In fact, it's often a serious challenge.

In most theatre production, the system calls for design conferences and design approval early in the creative process. So early that in many instances the show has yet to be cast, and almost never has it passed through the key stages of the rehearsal period. Once designs are approved, the director (and whoever else might be involved in the decision making) and the designers frequently go their separate ways with only minimal contact between two preparation teams: the actors and the director on the one hand and the designers and the shop crews on the other. Near the end of the rehearsal period, in the tech and dress rehearsals, these two teams come together for a final assimilation.

For anyone working in the American theatre, this system is so firmly entrenched, so familiar, so widely accepted, we seldom seriously question its inevitable weaknesses.

Under the present system, here is one of the key determiners of a production's quality: the skillful editing capacity of the key figures at the assembling stage. Too often, the desire is to use all or nearly all the creative work by the many contributors rather than to see what *now*—at this critical "assembly junction"—can be valuable in enhancing the play's experience for the actors and the audience. *And,* conversely, to see what *doesn't fit* as well as we thought it would when we came to an agreement those many days, sometimes weeks, ago.

For thirty years I worked in one of the most advanced performing arts centers on any college campus in America. My own productions and productions directed by my students were often designed by gifted artists and craftspeople who were both students and faculty members. In the years following, the best of those have earned considerable reputations for themselves throughout this country, working in film, television, and the living theatre. The opportunity for exhaustive experience (and I use the word *exhaustive* advisedly) in technical theatre in that program resulted in doors opening in the professional theatre and in theatre-related professions at a rate that was the envy of their peers in directing, acting, and playwriting. Yet the collaboration within that system was at best challenging. Much of that can be attributed to the kind of personality conflicts that occur in any large program demanding interplay of contributors. What stays with me, however, are incidents of differences in goals that seem symptomatic of the issue here, namely, the conflict between the vision and creation of the individual artist versus the needs of the whole. An example:

I vividly recall sitting mid-auditorium as we watched the costumed actors take their turns on stage under the lighting now set and gelled appropriately for the coming dress rehearsals. Beside me was a graduate student costume designer and beside him was his advisor. As the actors individually entered from the wings and took a position in the stage light, the costume mentor asked them to turn, take various positions, and add or remove accessories. The stage image was compared with the costume plates on the desk in front of us and the discussion focused on fittings, folds, and possible additions or removals.

Suddenly an actress entered who I hardly recognized. She sported not only the costume I had seen in the renderings, but a long, bright red wig. "Wooah!" I said. "What's that?" A long and spirited discussion ensued in which I learned that the intent was to replicate the hair color of the sketch so that it would match record photos of the production—photos that would be added to that designer's permanent portfolio in the soon to start career-long search for work.

I found myself stunned by the unexpected hurdle for the actress who had been making progress but was still far from secure in the role. I blurted out something like, "Those sketches were approved before we held tryouts! I did not cast a redhead!" Meanwhile, I watched the clearly uncomfortable actress on stage and projected her loss of confidence and her struggle to reestablish an identity in the little time remaining before opening. Eventually, the wig was discarded, but in my own mind the possibility that a costume sketch made prior to casting should take precedence over the needs of an actress on the eve of opening became a vivid reminder of a difference in priorities that may seldom be this obvious, but is likely to be present and must somehow be resolved as we struggle to create a consistent, believable, significant world.

Designers need to see the production's evolution happening as actors experience the play in rehearsal. When they cannot see it, directors need to be extremely sensitive to their own role in helping the designers reshape their designs so they contribute to the changing whole. And, finally, as part of the end game—those often exhausting tech and dress rehearsals—there is seldom enough time to seriously test the individual creations and their contribution to the whole. In the best of worlds, one might argue that there should *always* be as much time given to working with all the support elements in place as was given to rehearsal prior to tech and dress. Yes, I know, the out-of-town openings and preview runs—when they are built into the system—*can* be that time. Under the best of circumstances, they *may* occasionally be an exercise in collective creation of a high order. But how often does it work that way? When change is demanded, how prepared are the collaborators to see "the final edit" as their most creative time?

If it's true for the script, if it's true for the acting, isn't it also true for the support elements? Don't we need to reinforce the idea that dependent as we may sometimes be on skilled artists who can create pretty pictures, the final responsibility for any contribution's becoming a truly great design rests with *all* the collaborators? Working together, they must all see that the final assimilation of the production's many parts reinforce the whole—reinforce the core of the drama, contribute to its impact as a universal and significant human experience. Don't the training and the experience of all designers and builders need to make that axiomatic? If it's good, it needs to be more than pretty, it needs to help make the play *work*. To borrow from the medical profession: At the very least, it should do no harm. To be really great, it should be indispensable.

Here's why I believe the pretty-picture problem demands more attention today than ever: I believe one of the principal by-products of our computer workforce is that we are—in general—far more visually literate. Any interested middle-school student can produce impressive graphic design products using computer programs. We may not be producing great writers, but we certainly have a greater number of young people whose instincts have been nurtured and skills developed in the handling of visual elements of all kinds. Rare is the young person who is not intimately familiar with the complex images churned out constantly by the video game industry—and that is only the most obvious product of this newly developed visual (and audio) sensitivity in our culture.

I started this list of seven possibilities by suggesting that film and novels have had a far-reaching effect on our assumptions about the core of the theatre. Well…here is another: Our culture's current love affair with computer generated visuals has, it seems to me, further distracted us from the need for careful insistence on universal human experiences as the core of the living theatre.

In our eagerness to use the new toys, perhaps even as we recognize we can now provide mood and atmosphere, background and environment that are more elaborate and—at least sometimes—less expensive than those we could provide yesterday, don't we need to guard even more carefully against story and script changes and embellishments introduced primarily because we have the *means* to create them? Should we trust ourselves? We are, after all, a culture that walks through our neighborhoods while listening to our iPods—seeing and not seeing, listening and not listening. When do enhancements become the event? Isn't it shot through our culture?

A note from *Newsweek*, November 20, 2006: "'I can't say I understand it all, but it's going to be quite a ball park.' Fremont, California, Mayor Bob Wasserman, on high-tech plans for a new Oakland A's stadium that would let fans store e-tickets on cell phones, buy pictures of themselves and view instant replays at their seats."

Why would the theatre be an exception? If the game often becomes a secondary event in the skyboxes of the NFL and MLB, should we be surprised that our impulse is to make the theatre…well, what it too often has become?

Many would agree with me that Robert Edmond Jones was America's first great scene designer. His magnificent renderings

for O'Neill's plays are known to every serious student of the
theatre. His book *The Dramatic Imagination* became one of the
most widely read analyses written by anyone who worked in the
twentieth-century American theatre. Like many of his peers,
he challenged the theatre to reconsider the value of realistic
settings and the dominance of the picture-frame design that
began with forced perspective in the renaissance theatres. Yes,
we may, occasionally, still need to create the illusion of spaces
larger than the dimensions of our stages can hold, just as we
may sometimes need to shrink the performance spaces. But to
Jones and to many other mid-twentieth century theatre designers, the ability of film to provide real environments for stories
of human experiences seriously undercut the value of kitchen
sinks with running water and reconstructed living rooms with
one wall removed. In *The Dramatic Imagination* he told us,
"[T]he only theatre worth saving...is a theatre motion pictures
cannot touch." In that same work, he continued,

> It is a truism of theatrical history that stage pictures
> become important only in periods of low dramatic vi-
> tality. Great dramas do not need to be illustrated or
> explained or embroidered. They need only to be brought
> to life on the stage. The reason we have had realistic
> stage "sets" for so long is that few of the dramas of
> our time have been vital enough to be able to dispense
> with them. That is the plain truth. Actually the best
> thing that could happen to our theatre at this moment
> would be for playwrights and actors and directors to
> be handed a bare stage on which no scenery could be
> placed, and then told that they must write and act and
> direct for this stage.

It's not the intent here to advocate a specific style for design as insurance that we will create great theatre. I've seen
successful productions in too wide a range of styles to make
that assertion, despite my own preferences in sympathy with

much of Jones' concerns. What seems most to the point of this chapter is to recognize that the picture-frame stage, which continues to dominate our theatre, often causes designers (and the directors and actors who would use their work) to give less than adequate attention to the three dimensionality of a world with the human being at the center. Not only is the actor's world three dimensional, but it is—in the living theatre—a world that inevitably includes the audience as part of the event. For too long, we have tried to pretend that only the events inside a two-dimensional picture frame are experienced when we attend most living theatre productions. In so doing, we have not only overlooked enriching possibilities, but we have tried to pretend there is nothing outside that world that is registered by our senses as the performance progresses. It is as if the only thing we experience while sitting in the dentist's chair is what happens in the mouth where a spotlight shines from within the mirror overhead. Sitting in that dental chair, I, for one, am very aware of a whole world surrounding my teeth-framed action field. A world that includes an aching back, a partially masked face bending over me, my tightly crossed legs, and whatever I manage to focus on as I search the details of the room decoration, the joints and limbs of the dangling equipment, and the dimly visible comings and goings outside the window.

Quality design for the living theater will take into consideration all that extends, elaborates, emphasizes, clarifies, or distills the character for each of the actors by helping them meaningfully connect to the tasks that are part of the dramatic action of the play. It will help actors connect to each other in meaningful ways, help them connect to their environment, and help them connect to the audience. Moreover, the design will support our recognition of the key passages that take the characters and the audience through the changing events of the play. In short, design is not static. It is not limited to a picture in two dimensions with a carefully constructed frame—no matter how beautifully drawn or expertly photographed. What design can provide are the tools and the environment for seeing and hearing human beings more clearly, more definitively, as they carry out universal actions performed in the midst of an audience with whom they would share.

A pretty picture can capture or project a brief, chosen, partial moment in that connecting, sharing experience. It will never capture or project enough of the experience to insure great theatre without sustained and creative efforts by the director and the actors. There will—inevitably—be a lot of blanks to fill in. Blanks that only the human beings who are at the core of the play as it is performed *now* can provide.

It is that filling-in-the-blanks process that Jones addresses when he says, "...all art in the theatre should be not descriptive, but evocative. Not a description, but an evocation." Good design will help evoke a world and the connections within it. Connections that support the experiencing of the play—support its believability and its significance. Support the experiencing for the actors and support the experiencing for the audience.

Like great acting, great design will require considerable trial and error—trial and error that includes the human being at the center. The human being connecting.

Design work is not complete when the sketch is finished, not even when the setting or the costume is built. It takes the two hours of traffic on the stage before we know. It takes the play's passages to tell us. Only then will we find out how well we've designed the tools and the environment for our depiction of one of humankind's universal experiences. And don't be surprised when it needs some tinkering. If it's going to be a *great* design, expect it. Oh yes, and in the system, build in some time for the collaborative tinkering to happen. Some creative time. It will take more than our system has been willing to allot. More than we usually expect.

Almost always.

#7: Expand theatre architecture's role in connecting the actor and the audience.

CHOOSE SCRIPTS AND DEVELOP PRODUCTION SCHEMES THAT ENHANCE SHARED EXPERIENCE IN THE SPACES YOU NOW HAVE. CREATE NEW ARCHITECTURAL FORMS THAT ARE SIMPLE TO USE, DRAMATIC IN THEMSELVES, AND INVITE ACTOR-AUDIENCE EXCHANGE.

If this complex chapter title conjures up images of bricks and cement, glass and red carpets, let me be quick to say, "It's not about that." It's not about capital campaigns and teakwood floors either. Not about state-of-the-art performance palaces—not even about improvised, short-lived theatre spaces with plywood walls and dusty, velour drapes salvaged from the once-proud Ritz Theatre in the no-longer-respectable-neighborhood storefront with parking on the street if you dare.

What it's about is *memory*. It's about an unforgettable time.

You see, unlike film, the living theatre is an ephemeral art. Poof! It's gone. We've said it over and over on these pages: It's never the same twice. So, if you want it to last, what do you do? If you really believe the living theatre *can* be one of humankind's greatest tools—most indelible tools—for sharing human experiences, what do you do?

Well, you look for the special place. And what makes a place special? The connections it encourages and makes possible. Connections with our life story—the part we've nearly forgotten. Connections with those values and memories we care about most but seldom give full exposure. A place where we can find ourselves—again. Find who we are. Where we are going.

The special place: We get married there. We have the tough conversation there. We seek to be restored there. We remember there.

We drive across the country to stand in the midst of such a place. We hike, we march, we hold hands as we go through the door, through the trees, to the edge of the precipice. We are reminded of the roar of the crowd there. We know it happened there. There, we can be a child again. Our defenses are down. We can see there. Really see. And listen. Unbelievable. Once in a lifetime. Stunning. Bone deep.

There, we're free.

This chapter is about the importance of finding—creating—that magical, comforting, safe place. That sacred place where we invite the audience in to join us. To join us as we conjure spirits. As we create a time. As we remember. Together. As we tell how it was—and is. A place where we know you can be with us. Where you are a part of this story's being retold.

An unforgettable part. An indispensable part. Where we can experience it tonight—together.

It is, finally, the only thing the living theatre has to offer that film cannot do better. Otherwise...let it go. Let this form of re-creation go. Let the living theatre become what it appears headed for: a relic of the distant past.

To be worth saving, the living theatre must learn anew how to reconnect with its audience at this specific time, in this specific place—here.

Here. Now.

As I struggled with the ideas I sought to spell out in the preceding chapters, the presidential campaign of 2008 moved through the candidates' declarations of intent, the Iowa caucuses, the Super Tuesday primaries, the debates for candidates both Democrat and Republican, the narrowing of the field to John McCain, Hillary, and Barack, to the conventions in Denver and St. Paul, and to the intense final stretch, Sarah Palin days of October. Like many Americans, I listened to NPR news, became obsessed with television reports, read newspaper accounts and magazine articles, checked the internet sites daily—sometimes hourly—and experienced a roller coaster of elation and collapse, awe and disgust. I built stress and fatigue that could hardly have been greater had I been among the press corps going from stop to stop through city after city, state after state—red, blue, and undecided.

On November 4 I voted.

That afternoon, I typed out the first draft of a title and the first few sentences for this seventh and final chapter. I looked at my watch and stopped, and a few minutes later my wife and I turned on the television set. With dinner in our laps, we joined the hundreds of millions worldwide who sat and paced, snacked and sipped, waiting.... Waiting, flipping from MSNBC to CNN and back again as the painfully slow results moved from the East toward the West. We thought we knew—if we were to believe the polls—and yet....

We have only a few of those times in our lives. Only a few such unforgettable gatherings. High drama—and we, like nearly everyone else, felt the tension that proved it. The polls closed on the West Coast and the networks made it official. Or at least as official as television commentators can make it. Barack Obama was to be the forty-fourth president of the United States.

And then it happened: We watched as tens of thousands sprinted past the barricades to be part of the celebration in Grant Park, Chicago, and we too were there. Even as we watched from our living room, we were there.

I suspect I will long retain many of those images from that night. Most of you who read this will remember, as I do, not just the president-elect and his family—Michelle in her black and red dress, those two young girls dancing out to stand before the crowd—not just the Obamas, but all the eager, upturned, beaming faces of person after person in the throng before that stage, the towering skyline of Chicago behind them. A few of those faces were recognizable and famous, but most were unknown and yet equally arresting, for they were all crying and laughing, their arms around one another, their eyes wide. Shouting. Singing. Crying and laughing faces of those who needed to be there. People who will—for as long as they live—tell others what it felt like to be part of that Grant Park experience: Grant Park, the night Barack Obama became the first black president of the United States.

This chapter is about the uniqueness of the living theatre: the ability to make the audience a part of each performance. If we doubt the significance of that connection, remember life's most powerful moments. How badly we need to share our incredible times with one another. It's something we must never forget if the living theatre is to survive. It's the one quality that distinguishes the living theatre from film and the recorded-image dramatic arts. Something we have somehow—in our infatuation with technology—nearly forgotten.

During my lifetime of work in the theatre, nothing surprised me more than the lack of significant change in theatre

architecture. There are exceptions, of course, and we'll come
to those shortly. But first let me say that few would dispute
the generalization that the proscenium theatre still dominates
American theatre architecture.

To me, the nearly impossible theatre space, found in high
schools, civic buildings, community theatres, and colleges
throughout America, is a proscenium theatre. It seats from six
hundred to two thousand people in its parallel rows where heads
crane left and right to see past the inevitably taller before us.
It has a thirty-foot opening (more or less), a fly loft with ropes
and pulleys, a limited off-stage space (fifteen feet to the wall
from the arch if you're lucky), a stage elevated from three to
four feet above the front rows of the auditorium, and audience
seating raked—if at all—by fifteen or fewer degrees. Mix in the
usual limited, if not altogether missing, shops for set building,
and producers and directors have a challenge indeed. And yet,
ask most Americans if there are theatre buildings in their community, the answer will be "yes," and these are the spaces to
which they will refer us. These are our "real" theatres.

And, yes, our Broadway theatres are proscenium theatres
and each of them has at least some of the pitfalls outlined
above.

In 1967 I went to Montreal to an international symposium
on theatre architecture. The most celebrated names in the
world theatre were among the speakers. Expo 67 was in full
sway, and its breathtaking spaces showcased some of the most
impressive displays of creative interplay between filmmakers
and architects seen before or since. In Europe, the rebuilding
following the terrible destruction of World War II had spawned
a wide array of theatre forms that were the talk of theatre
people everywhere. In the United States, the Ford Foundation
paired architects with directors and designers, resulting in the
widely praised *The Ideal Theatre: Eight Concepts*, a diverse set
of designs that appeared to be ushering in a new era of performance spaces. Lincoln Center, the Kennedy Center, the Arena
Stage, the Alley Theatre, the Music Center in Los Angeles,

the Krannert Center at the University of Illinois, the Guthrie Theatre in Minneapolis, and a handful of others seemed to be pointing the way.

So, what happened? Why do we seldom have a "Grant Park" in our theatre experience? And why do those proscenium theatres keep going and going and going?

First, a confession: I have long had a special interest in theatre architecture. More specifically, I have had a special interest in the use of space in the theatre. My doctoral dissertation examined the spatial relationship between the actor and the audience in the productions of three directors, Max Reinhardt, Tyrone Guthrie, and Nicholai Okhlopkov. And yes, I know, if I were reading someone else's chapters, bells would likely be going off right now. "Beware," they would say, "another academic with a thesis on the shelf who is still trying to justify the time it took to write the thing—a thesis so narrow, only he cares about it."

Well, part of that is true. Certainly, I do care about it. And, certainly, that project played a significant role in determining the path of my theatre career—more than that, my life. To some degree, I suppose I *am* a bit defensive about my enthusiasm. Try as I might, I find myself rewriting this chapter again and again, trying to dampen my likely overstatements. Unlike many dissertations undertaken because of the prodding of an advisor or a topic chosen from a practical but less than soulful concern, the work of those three directors involved ideas and practices I found fascinating fifty years ago and I find fascinating now. Moreover, I spent four decades finding ways to expand my understanding of the possibilities for the effective use of space in the theatre. During that time I may have had as much experience creating productions and supervising others' directing efforts in a range of spaces as varied as anyone who has worked in the theatre—spaces of all kinds, theatres and non-theatres. Spaces formed by nature and spaces built for protecting and working and sharing. Spaces built to keep people out and to bring people in. And not one of those experiences dimmed my belief that space counts—enormously. Quite the opposite.

If, as a young man, I found the director's use of theatrical space intriguing, I now find myself convinced that how we use space, how we promote or inhibit actor and audience connection within it, is so central to the memorable living theatre experience that our skill in handling that connection will determine whether the living theatre survives as a significant art form.

However—why we have been so slow to understand and accept that importance I now believe to be far more complex than I recognized at the beginning of my career.

Let's look again at the evolution of film and the parallel evolution of the theatre. The proscenium still dominates theatre architecture, even as more and more film viewing moves into our living rooms with larger and larger flat-screen television sets, while Blu-ray and DVD recording battle it out for our drama dollars. Going to the movies as a communal experience seems to be eroding as the preferred tactic for film viewing. Meanwhile, many of our living theatres are a half to three-quarters of a century old and were built when film was taking its cues from the theatre and not the reverse. Since then, when film came to clearly dominate our theatre culture, and even movie theatres underwent significant changes in their architectural form—and, yes, I'm thinking of the TenPlex versus the old Rialto, one of which stands empty on a corner three blocks from us—we still built proscenium theatres again and again that are all too much like the Rialto. In fact, to add insult to injury, we have taken more than a few of those old Rialto theatres and "given" them to the local community theatre (maybe even the local resident professional theatre), expecting them to be grateful for the good fortune that produced a here-it-is-and-now-stop-your-whining-and-make-something-of-it home. If you're looking for a home for your theatre company and want a challenge, there it is.

I know. Not all proscenium theatres are alike. And not all of them are awful. In fact, over a twenty-five-year span I directed productions in one I would rank among *the very best*, and, yes, it made possible some wonderful experiences. But it was and is among the rare exceptions, and all of us who worked there knew it.

But here is the second part of my personal confession: I long ago concluded that it was not the architect or the engineer who was responsible for creating new and more stimulating theatre forms—not even the scene designer or the tech director, no matter how knowledgeable they might be about grid heights and inches between seat rows. Believing so strongly that where we bring the actor and the audience together and how we design their interaction is at the core of the living theatre's very ability to survive—and finding so little current evidence of a significant number of others who share my concern—it takes all my energy to keep the demon in the box: Yes, part of me wants to grab any director I encounter and shout, "It's not someone else's job, it's *yours*! Pay attention! You're the one who must learn how to use space. Not someone else—*you*!

"Don't for a second think the architects and the boards of directors are going to save you! Don't look to the playwrights. Don't look to the designers. If you want a theatre that counts, *you* must pay attention to space. Yes, I know you've learned the script counts. Yes, I know you believe the actor counts. Well, here—for the director—is the third absolutely essential study: The space where we come together. If you want the living theatre to become an unforgettable part of our experiences, if you want it to play a significant role in shaping our lives, you must become far more sensitive to the enormity of our spatial options as we seek to connect our audiences and our created worlds."

If we want the living theatre to offer a more powerful experience than the film and its descendants can provide, here is the first and most important learning: Space counts, and every director needs to become a student, open to continually learning about space as he or she goes about the experiences of life day after day. Space counts, and your familiarity with those endlessly repeated proscenium-floorplan templates with their DRs and DCs and ULs will not do it!

You must study how we feel when we are together in a space. How our feelings change when we can see each other and when we can't. When we are close to one another and when we are not. When the space makes you seem small and when it makes you seem enormous. When you seem so far above me, so far away from me, you are no longer in my world. How our relationship changes when you come down to my level, down to be with me, to share what I see, sharing what I feel now.

You must sit quietly alone in your theatre, before you move your actors from their rehearsal rooms into that space. You must sit and imagine possibilities. Again and again, you must come back into your theatre and consider what you have not yet done to reveal the values of that space. See what else could be possible. See how its revelations can be scored, holding back that cross until it is most affecting, avoiding the obvious, surprising us, making our world seem smaller and more oppressive, making it seem larger and more freeing. Making that space seem more freeing than we ever thought possible—thought possible, *here*.

You must become a composer. A sculptor in space.

And you must do it again and again after you make the actor transfer. After it is your cast's new home. You must come back alone and sit, with only that light and then another. Returning again after you have experienced it with an audience. After you see—and *feel*—what it is like to be there with the witnesses. You must sit *here*, and then sit *there*, and then *over there*. You must sit, remembering. Remembering and seeing what is possible.

For too long we have set the play in one space, the audience in another, a window between. Born of the discovery of perspective drawing, that concept was given new life when we built our faux living rooms and our faux kitchens and, ripping down our fourth walls, allowed audiences to peek through—to be present and yet not present. When we allowed our re-creations to go on as if independent of those who came to see. "Don't violate that fourth wall," we said. "Pretend they aren't watching."

And somehow, in the confusing, simultaneous evolution of the living stage and the once almost incidental, but soon burgeoning industry of motion pictures—somehow, as we hung our movie frame on the wall and watched the flickering images within—it became easy to forget. To forget the vitality that comes from the connection, the real, physical connection between the actor and the audience. To forget the power of the actor who walks among us.

Occasionally, the novelty of that window between spaces as a unique viewpoint for the living theatre may heighten the dramatic experience—occasionally. But isn't it time to stop making it the default choice? Let's remember, the living theatre brings us together. We go to see and hear one another. To connect. To interact with one another. Let us find ways to get those who tell the story in contact with those who are the witnesses, those who come together to see and hear its being told. Let the witnesses to that story be part of our memory. "I only am escaped alone to tell thee." Archibald MacLeish gave that line to the witness of the story of J.B.—to the story of Job. In every telling of the story there's a witness. The one who saw. Who saw as only he could see.

When we go to the theatre, let us remember not only the victim and the killer, not only the one who left and the one left behind, but the one who saw it. She who saw and was deeply moved. In every great performance, there will be those among us, those in the audience, who see and are moved in a way no one else is moved. Or so it will seem to each of us. And in our memories those people will become as vital a part of the keepings as Oedipus. As Barack.

We will feel their responses alongside us—feel their responses validating our own. We will see their tears; hear their laughter; remember their gasps of amazement. The stakes will be elevated because they were there with us. Because we were one—among them.

We must learn to bring the action out into the audience, through the audience, among the audience, interacting with the audience, not because it is clever, not to attract attention to itself, but because it is the inevitable, obvious extension of the re-creation of the action of the play. Because the world of the play does not stop at the edge of the stage, because the play's world and the audience's world are one, with no cliff separating them where the actors peer out into the meaningless void. The living theatre must create a world—one world—where the audience is invited in. Where the play happens and we, too, are part of it. Quietly, perhaps. Sitting in a corner, perhaps. Ducking for cover if necessary. Where those in the audience can be enlisted if an extra pair of hands is needed to hold a glass of water or a child's outstretched fingers—not because it is cute or clever, but because that is what would be expected of us were we the same well-intentioned witnesses on a street corner or a bus, in a supermarket or a department store.

Of course the couple before us has a disagreement. Of course we are unexpectedly exposed to the fear or the panic or the joy of the moment's terrible urgency by someone we had never before seen—but haven't such things happened to us as we waited for our plane or our change or our car to be brought from the parking lot? Haven't people there been suddenly aware that we were listening, that they were being seen by another? Haven't they acknowledged our presence, spoken to us, apologized to us, and instantly returned to their task? "What are you looking at?" they've said. "I'm sorry," they've said. "He's like that," they've said. And back they go. Back into their argument. Back to get it done. Grabbing their fellow actor by the lapel with little regard for us onlookers, or all too aware that we onlookers made all the difference, and that our witnessing meant their words challenged the weight of a culture's beliefs.

Of course this happens in our lives—in our daily lives. We do not live alone. Our most affecting moments occur, as often as not, among other people. Should we not expect it in the theatre? Why would we want an audience to see the play with us if we do not want the comfort, the reassurance, the power of other witnesses to remind us this is how life works?

In the great performances, we will remember them all: hero, villain, he who was there as part of the story, and she who was there with us. She who sat over there. She who seemed to be holding her breath. She who watched, oh so lovingly, as the actor reached out and touched the cheek of her daughter sitting beside her. She who was part of that night when we too were moved. She who will always be part of our memory of that special time in that special place.

We do not go to the living theatre to witness the event alone. We go to share.

Here's a simple test for the memorable living theatre event: If you—you in the cast and you in the audience—come home from the experience and cannot remember at least one other face reacting to the power of the play, if that person's reaction is not intimately tied to your storing up the images of the night, wait for the film. The movie will be a more memorable experience. And if there is no movie, read the novel.

So. What *about* the architecture?

In a few theatres, connecting the actor and the audience will seem nearly impossible. In others it will seem almost inevitable. But make no mistake: To make actor and audience interaction a valuable part of the experience requires a director who understands the value of that connection and actors who are open to learning the benefits of the best of these experiences. In reality, in no theatre is it impossible to short-circuit the potential power of the exchange. As audience members or actors we can isolate ourselves. We can resist human connection. We do it in our daily lives and certainly we can do it in the theatre. What makes a space easy or difficult to use, successful or unsuccessful in connecting the audience with the performance, is as open to subjective judgment as any other question of style. In short, use it well and it's a good space. Use it poorly and it's

not. Nevertheless, here are some considerations worth thought-
ful attention.

Let's begin with one of the most obvious questions. How
large a theatre do you need? In America we tend to see bigger as
better. In the living theatre, that's seldom true. When in doubt,
go smaller. Yes, large-scale events—a rock concert, a football
game—may gain stature from the frenzy of the energized
mob. A public protest, a parade, a political event may remind
us there are many who share our beliefs. And, occasionally, in
the theatre a huge throng may add to the production's power.
But such theatre experiences are extremely rare and will almost
always demand special attention to preserve the humanity of
the central characters. Closed-circuit, large-screen, simultaneous projections can give us close-ups of faces, but their impact
diminishes quickly, and at the core of the work is this simple
reality: The human scale is determined by the size of a live person who is among us. Place him where we can see him. Let us
see his interactions with other human beings. The living theatre
profits from a house where a high percentage of the audience
is close to the action. Today, in those instances where a theatre
company produces in theatres of distinctly different sizes, the
larger theatre is almost always marketed and perceived as the
more important one. It is where the production budget is largest
and where the more experienced—and presumably better—directors work. I suggest those larger theatres are likely to be the
ones where it is more difficult to create effective connections
with the audience. Wouldn't it be a significant step forward for
theatre organizations if we were to market our smaller spaces
as our preferred theatres? Wouldn't it make a difference if we
believed it?

Another rule of thumb I believe in: A one-time dramatic
event has its own spontaneous, unpredictable drama. A living
theatre performance to be repeated again and again—as most
are—will almost always reach consistently higher standards if
the audience capacity is a bit smaller than demand. There is
enormous value in a full house—no matter how small the audi-

torium. Those unconscious factors at work, for both actors and audiences, are difficult to deny even if we can't always define them. The energy, the focus gained by having all available seats filled, adds significantly to our belief that the event is worth our time. "Sold out" is not only a boon financially, but a significantly positive contribution to everyone's perception of the experience.

And that seems like the cue for a look at our second most popular theatre: the black box. The idea behind the black box is admirable: a relatively small space where, for each production, we can design not only the playing area, but the audience space. Where the seating can be shaped around the action most any way we choose. Where the action can weave into and through the audience at this level and that. Or at least that's what some of us believed we were doing when we first created such spaces shortly after the mid-twentieth century. We created a theatre where the design for a production included the whole enchilada. In my own case, it was Nicholas Okhlopkov's 1930s work at the Realistic Theatre in Moscow that served as my model. Okhlopkov tore out a proscenium and its seating and in that box developed some wonderful floorplans and highly acclaimed productions—so successful they earned him a trip to Siberia from Joseph Stalin. I never saw those productions, but photos of the work and descriptions of the audiences' experiences were part of the study for that dissertation I wrote those many years ago. It was enough to cause me to create a flexible space of my own at the first opportunity, with platform modules for seating—squares and rectangles with attachable legs of various heights. More modest than most of the theatres I was to work in later, it was still one of the most satisfying.

The key to that theatre was our willingness to spend the time and energy required shaping the playing space to fit the action of each play and, in turn, shaping the audience seating around and through those playing areas. Even for an audience of a hundred or so, it involved considerable time and energy, but directing and designing there taught me a great deal about audience interaction.

Okhlopkov's work is largely unknown in this country, but in the sixties there were significant others. The designs of Jerzy Grotowski's Polish Lab Theatre stood New York critics on their heads, and the sets by Jerry Rojo for the productions of Richard Schechner's Performance Garage may have been upstaged by the nudity in those productions, but for anyone interested in theatre's use of space, they were remarkable. A few people will remember that even Broadway saw a truly environmental setting when *Candide* made the move from the Brooklyn Academy of Music to the Broadway Theatre in the early seventies. Then, of course, there were all those off-off-Broadway storefront productions that fit seating into nooks and crannies of unlikely spaces wherever they could be found—a tradition that still exists across the country.

Out of all this emerged the black box theatre form, an architect-designed theatre usually built alongside the primary theatre space, which was almost always a proscenium house, but occasionally a thrust stage. That black box form is now seen on college campuses and as part of many American regional theatres scattered across the country.

From my view, that innovation should have had a more positive influence on the theatre than it has had. But almost immediately, two significant limiting practices emerged: First, we sought to standardize seating arrangements in order to shorten the time and reduce the effort required to set up for each production. Some form of bleacher seating became the order of the day, large banks of relatively easy-to-move risers where chairs could be added. True, these risers can be arranged on one, two, three, or four sides, but few would argue that the seat banks are in any way conducive to easy interaction between actor and audience. At their worst, they produce end-stage arrangements where steep banks of audience faces line up in rigid parallel rows facing a flat floor on which a few set pieces provide an environment for the action.

Our second limiting practice was to turn over many, if not most, of these theatres to beginners. Too many black box theatres have become theatre laboratories with little experience to guide the work. Granted, young would-be directors and designers are often willing to take risks, are sometimes exceptionally talented, and may spend time and energy to make something of little, but if black box theatres are to have a significant impact on theatre standards, the people working there need more inspirational models. They need adequate budgets and shop time. And—of course—they need better alternatives to those defeating, clumsy seat banks.

The black box form requires not less, but more sophisticated understanding of the design of the playing space, and a careful set of decisions about the best viewpoints to arrange the seating in relation to the action. In short, there may be less conventional scenery required for a black box than we usually demand for our proscenium stages, but to use the form well, we need an even better insight into design.

The most encouraging work I've seen recently in an American black box theatre was at the Oregon Shakespeare Festival in Ashland. The productions were consistently among their very best offerings, well cast from the resident company, well designed, and adequately budgeted. By comparison with the productions in their two larger houses, one a proscenium and the other a faux Old Globe—this last a very difficult theatre for audience-actor connection because of its size and the lack of a significant thrust for the open stage—the black box productions seemed to profit from the smaller space and the actors' enjoyment of the ease with which they could relate to one another and to the audience. Especially impressive was the fact that the productions were performed in rotating repertory where playing spaces and audience seating banks were rearranged from day to day. The seat banks remain seat banks, however, with little opportunity for any actor movement among the rows of seated audience members.

One other common practice in black box theatres should be mentioned: the use of the grid and catwalks. Almost all architect-designed black boxes are basically simple in form and relatively economical to build. The one lavish investment included in many is a lighting system with an elaborate overhead grid and catwalk balconies that are hung above the audience on three or four sides of the space, providing access to lighting instruments and control positions for light and sound operation. In many productions, those overhead passages have become a welcome means of expanding the playing space. What their use suggests is that the adventuresome director will include almost any available space as a playing area, given the opportunity. Not always, of course, will those uses contribute to the quality of the production, but it is a reminder that, for many, the willingness to explore the space is real. For the future, what is more urgently needed is a better understanding of the value of using those spaces to connect actor and audience.

Let's look at script choice and its implications for these spatial forms and for actor-audience relationships. Two major categories come to mind: the number of people in the cast and the number of locales called for to carry out the dramatic action.

Today, the one-person show is enjoying an unprecedented popularity—at least unprecedented in my lifetime. It's probably accurate to say economic reality has been the major factor contributing to its familiarity. Not only does it limit the payroll cost for actors who must be supported by a production, but it clearly simplifies the rehearsal process. Much of the usual rehearsal work can be carried out with little time in a conventional rehearsal space and sometimes without a director or a tech crew of any kind.

But what a one-person show demands is that the actor develop significant skill in relating to an audience—a quality I believe in short supply among our acting pool members. And, in fact, it is here the influence of the one-person show may have the best opportunity to help us develop insight into theatre architecture and its role in raising the quality of the living theatre.

The actor in the one-person show, the storyteller, the singer, the stand-up comedian, the public speaker—all remind us that in their best work not only will the audience be able to see and hear the performer, but the performer will be able to see and hear the audience. As subtle as their continuing interaction may sometimes be, it will play a major role in the effect of the presentation.

This truism was brought home to me in an unusual experience, perhaps worth retelling. Several years ago I had created and directed a version of Shakespeare's *Romeo and Juliet* in which we retained the original text but edited it somewhat and inserted narration at a dozen or so points in a style not unlike the narration given to the Stage Manager in Wilder's *Our Town*. This time the narration provided historical insights into the London of Shakespeare's era and the conditions under which the play was created. At the last minute I decided to play the newly created storyteller role and, to simplify the casting, to make it part of the production's style to have that character also assume the role of the prince and a number of the smaller servant roles as they occurred in the course of the play. The result of the insertions and the editing was a reduction of the total cast to about fifteen or so actors.

Even so, it felt like a large production. What with flashing swords and close-up film projection of actors and the like, it clearly filled the 650-seat proscenium house. The forestage had been raised with the hydraulic lifts, pushing the apron out well beyond the curtain line, with the caliper stages left and right providing for additional exits and entrances.

As I went out on the forestage in the midst of the audience each night, I was reminded of the power of Guthrie's thrust stage to make possible the contact between the actor and the audience before him. And then, one night, an extraordinary thing happened: We lost all electrical power due to a severe thunderstorm. Emergency lights came on and we stopped the production, sending the audience out into the common lobby where several of the other performances' viewers were gathering on the vast teakwood floor. Eventually, we actors joined them as well as we all waited to see if the productions and concerts might be able to resume. Finally, someone appeared with the damage report suggesting it could be morning before power was restored. A decision was made to give refunds to those who would like to leave but to resume the several presentations with emergency lighting for those who would like to stay. With that we returned to our backstage places and readied our play for the next scene.

A number of additional candelabra were pulled from the prop room, candles were lit, and as the audience settled into their seats, I made my way out onto the forestage and began the next piece of narrative to pick up where we had lost power.

Suddenly, I became aware of this absolutely extraordinary silence. I was standing in the same place I had stood on nights before, but I was able to see and—more importantly—hear that audience in a way I had never experienced before. There was not the slightest movement by *anyone* in that house I could not hear. Whatever contact I had had with them or their predecessors seemed totally superficial compared with what was before me now. As I stood there I suddenly realized why. The air exchange system that pumped warmed or cooled air to this enormous set of boxes housing a concert hall, three theatres, and a lobby only slightly smaller than a football field, along with myriad offices and a spate of rehearsal rooms, was no longer rumbling beneath our feet. No one in that audience could make the slightest movement without my hearing it. And—I could see. There were no spotlights in my eyes, and even in the dim light I could see any face I chose from those before me. But it was the silence I remember. A silence that connected us as I sought the expectant eyes in one face after another.

I have no doubt it was the best performance I gave in the role, and I have never forgotten the potential for connecting when the actor can really see—and really *hear*—any audience member she chooses in the audience before her. Much of the connection it takes to make a performance special may well depend on subtleties as simple as the quiet in the theatre that spring night. The quiet—and a thrust stage that put me in what seemed like the very center of the upturned faces. On a special night, after the storm.

Guthrie's thrust stage theatre at Stratford was such a success in the fifties it brought all of Europe running to see what was possible in creating a new home for Shakespeare. It completely dwarfed the work at Stratford, Connecticut, where America's own Shakespeare festival opened in a new proscenium theatre that spent the next several years trying to find ways to adapt its stage with thrusts and aprons, to little avail—a theatre built with materials and accessories that would be envied by most, but that today stands empty and unused.

The thrust stage Guthrie and his designer, Tanya Moiseiwitsch, created for Stratford, Ontario, with its architectural setting, its multiple platforms and *vomitori*, allowing for exits and entrances under the front rows of the audience, became the model for the theatre built in Minneapolis. This time, the intent was to prove its form could serve more than the plays of Shakespeare—to prove it could bring the classics to the heartland of America. From its first seasons, plays by the likes of Miller, Moliere, and Chekhov were included. Who would have guessed that Chekhov could be mounted on an open stage? And yet *Three Sisters* here was a rousing success.

But the theatre seated nearly 1,500 people and after Guthrie's departure, sustaining audiences was a challenge. In the ensuing years, the urge for changes of setting to go with changes of script proved irresistible. There were several attempts to create smaller theatres for the company's use and there were several changes in leadership. Where the Stratford theatre was once celebrated for its architectural setting, the Minneapolis theatre soon resorted to elaborate settings as new productions of differing styles were mounted. Over the years, they struggled to rebuild audiences and find the right match of repertoire, theatre spaces, and audience interest. Finally, a new complex with three theatres was designed to replace their original home, and in 2006 it opened.

The new facility included not only a remake of the original house with its wraparound auditorium complete with varied colored seats—the original Guthrie's architect, Ralph Rapson, wanted them to better compensate for empty seats should they occur—but also a proscenium theatre, said by artistic director Joe Dowling to be more suitable to the "full range of the extraordinary American repertoire." Today, according to the promotional material of the Guthrie: "Although a thrust stage works brilliantly for Shakespeare and other large-scale plays, more contemporary plays focusing on the subtleties of characters' psychological development require a smaller proscenium stage. [In our new complex] a proscenium features a 'picture frame' rectangular opening, allowing the entire audience to experience the play from the same vantage point—straight on, a perspective not possible on a thrust stage. The majority of the late 19th century and virtually all of 20th-century drama is best suited to a proscenium stage."

Even more telling, the most celebrated architectural feature of the new Guthrie is not the form of the theatres themselves, nor any production innovation, but its "Endless Bridge," a cantilevered extension of the lobby that juts out 78 feet towards the river, "providing an unparalleled view of sunsets over the Mississippi."

Perhaps it only again makes clear how easily our design focus is shifted from the essentials to packaging—even when it comes to the extremely costly choices for the theatre's architecture. For decades we were preoccupied with the "stage house" and its provisions for shifting scenery. Today, we know we can provide background with projections that is within the capacity of most high-school-age young artists. We know we can evoke place with selected set pieces and light. We know that multi-platforms can allow us to go from one room to another or one city to another, from one time to another. That light and shadow can focus on one space and hide others until we need them. We know that cast sizes vary enormously and the amount of playing space needed to carry out the physical action for one play can be totally inappropriate for another. We know that among the script forms having the highest production frequency are one-person shows and musicals, two forms where the performers directly address the audience—even if the old admonition "just focus above the heads of the audience" is still frequent advice used to protect the nervous actor from the unsettling gaze of the viewers.

But we also know that if the money can be found, most productions will spend lavishly on costumes, settings, and properties—and, now we learn, when it comes to theatre architecture, we'll retreat to the familiar proscenium while we use our innovative dollars on the sunset view at intermission.

And so here we are—again.

What is the ideal theatre, given the reality of today's living theatre art? Well, certainly it isn't any one architectural form. It has become painfully clear that no matter how attractive or functional a space may be to some, or even most, if those who are attempting to produce there aren't ready or willing to find its potential, its use can only be disappointing.

It is difficult to engineer change when it comes to spaces. Buildings are expensive. Some, ridiculously expensive. Once built, once we've signed the mortgage, it's not easy to throw it out and start again. But no building is really ours until we've lived in it. Until we've found out what serves us well. There are always surprises. Once you get a glimpse of the incredible life it's possible to create there, with work, we have the possibility of learning how it can be reignited. Yes, we're often envious of those with new toys, and who wouldn't want great artists around who can build new things—things you've never had a chance to try? But don't forget the discoveries learned under the steps. Somehow, those discoveries will work their way into another creation if they are powerful enough—because this is where they live. Where the memory of them lives.

Personally, after years of belief in a flexible, environmental space, there was a time when I thought if I were starting over, I might not choose to own a space at all—only a package of portable equipment. That's not because I didn't still believe in the idea of an empty space where audience as well as playing areas, *along with their relationships*, were carefully designed for each production. No, I wasn't rejecting that idea, I only wondered if it didn't require more time and energy than we could usually manage in the day's cultural climate. To choose already existing spaces and bring in lights, sound, and the rest that can be set up in the found environment, wherever the subject and the audience takes us, is really the same idea, but an attempt at reducing the size of the task. That's what much of Reinhardt's later career depended on, and it was certainly something that served me well during many of my most memorable efforts. Few stagings left me with more stimulating memories than our having set up shop for a performance on the floor of the Chicago Stock Exchange, after all. A performance where audience seating circled the pits and actors ran and shouted through key events from the life of Lincoln while the financial numbers of the day flashed overhead.

No, I don't believe there can be a single answer to the search for the ideal space—certainly not one space for all productions and all who would work there—but instead I believe there is a need to evolve new spaces by giving far more conscious attention to the spatial relationships in every production, wherever it is realized. In short, I think we get there a discovery at a time.

For me, it was a major learning experience to direct on an outdoor stage. The theatre we built for our company's beginning effort owed considerable debt to Guthrie and Moiseiwitsch and their architectural setting at Stratford. But nothing had prepared me for the effect of the perfect night sky as we played out the final battles of the Civil War or the first landing on the moon on that outdoor stage. And the plays we created for that space were also performed in an enormous range of found spaces with their own historical auras, and that led to the creation of new pieces especially for performance at other historic sites.

But our company's last theatre, and for me our best, had an inauspicious beginning. It was a smaller indoor theatre built to show an orientation film for our historic site home and, as a secondary service, it was to provide our theatre's emergency space, a bad weather retreat from the larger, more complex stage of the outdoor theatre. It also functioned as a temporary home while the outdoor theatre was razed and rebuilt with much more sophisticated amenities for both audience and actors.

The new indoor theatre was sketched out on the proverbial napkin when I was faced with the architect's projected conventional rectangle of a proscenium arch space. I was lucky. Not only did the architect use all the basic elements of the drawing I hastily produced and later detailed to beat review deadlines, but he added finishings of his own that helped create a simple, imminently versatile two-hundred seat theatre that I came to love. It was built on a diagonal axis within a square floor plan. Its architectural stages and background required no major construction, but only set decoration and selective lighting, with projections when needed, to beautifully serve everything from one person shows through realistic American dramas to our historical epics with casts of fifteen playing through nearly fifty scenes, which were scattered before and around us on the side stages and balconies with assorted levels encircling the audience. In the end, that little theatre became my long-sought home.

Of all the theatres I have known, none—to me—was more beloved than that space. So much so that today, were I to have that theatre in Southern California, I suspect I would still be directing, despite my all too clear understanding of the energy required to rebuild a company, to find an audience, and to generate the finances necessary to keep the work going. It would not satisfy all theatre productions, I know, but for an amazing array of scripts and production styles, I found it so very, very easy to use. So simple it sometimes felt like we were cheating.

And for me, and for many in our audiences, it was an absolutely beautiful space to enter.

And that brings me to the only conclusion I find possible for the search outlined in this chapter: Of all the elements of the theatre, I have come to believe the evolution of a "home" is the most elusive. Yes, it is a major investment with all the fund-raising and financial preoccupation that entails. And yet I am convinced it's central to our understanding of the way up. If we are to pull ourselves out of the muck by our bootstraps, we have to develop a new model for the very image of a theatre: not only the theatre performance but the space where we come together to share what happens.

And, I believe, few who work in today's theatre are ready to build it.

Those few new individual theatres that have been successful have consistently been upgrades of an evolved space. The Arena Stage in Washington, D.C. is a case in point. Left to draw on our own insights, most decision makers who have the opportunity to create a new home for the living theatre will fall back on someone else's advice: architects, engineers, audience developers, accessory artists who know about carpeting and maybe even acoustics, but who lack real understanding of both the core of the theatre and of human connections.

Somehow, we need to bury the belief that the ideal theatre is a neutral room where we line people up in rows, one behind the other, stretching back hundreds of feet from a picture on the wall. Black box, plush red seats, marble or teak walls: such a space seldom feeds the soul.

Yes, some argue—still—that lining up those rows allows us all to see the same images in the frame before us. But we never do, of course, rows one behind the other or not. Even if the telephoto lens has seduced us into believing the experience from the last row is the same as from the first, *my* experience tells me that is never true. Never.

It's not easy to see quality work done in new and stimulating theatre models—in *really* new theatre forms. And I believe it's absolutely true that few of us have had the opportunity to develop tools to use a new space well. Probably it's even more basic than that: Probably, few of us have made such a learning one of our higher priorities. Yes, we know how difficult it is to finance a new theatre. We understand how difficult it is to sustain the audiences that will keep the seats filled. What we don't recognize is how little we know about space. To develop models that will guide us, we need opportunities to feel the difference. Firsthand. We need to find ways to store it up in our subconscious.

We need new ways of thinking about a theatre space at its simplest. I have tried to challenge the picture on the wall as our default model. For centuries one of the simplest images for a theatre was "two boards and a passion"—a platform set up in the public square. Maybe we need to return to that, asking, "Where do we set up the platform?" And maybe the next questions are, "Can we find a space where we already have a platform? Where we have several platforms? Some for the action and some where the audience can sit so they can better see?" Yes, I know: We need lights and masking; we need quiet and dressing rooms and rest rooms. Yes, yes. But what is really essential? What is essential, *now*?

Maybe one of our most useful models for a theatre that might save us is our living room—our own where-we-live room. No, not literally; not the small living room of your home and mine, although that isn't an impossibility, but a place, nevertheless, where we could move the furniture around as needed. Yes, we can push the chairs over there for this one. We don't need that hallway for the actors this time. And we can dim the lights or even pull the panels closed to shut off the observatory.

Remember *Vanya on 42nd Street*? Andre Gregory's wonderful film shot in the decaying lobby and spaces of a condemned Broadway theatre? It really began by getting actors together in a living room, and the final product shared that feeling.

I do think we need to invite our audiences into our "home." Maybe not two boards and a passion in a town square, but in our "home" where we could get to know our guests. Where we could listen to their stories. Where we could seat them amid hospitable surroundings and before them, in their midst, begin the play.

Imagine: The action takes place to their side, behind them, above them on the balcony or the stairs; people enter from the basement, from the front door, or from the hall—and depending on the demands of tomorrow's play we could move the chairs, using this space for some in the audience today, using it for the actors gathering around the table tomorrow.

Am I the only one who sees far more creative restaurant interiors and hotel lobbies than theatres? Maybe we should choose some of the most interesting ones and use them as our theatre models. Why is it most theatres remind me of the coach seating section of a jumbo jet? My body feels about the same after an hour or two in either of those environments.

"Surely the first step toward creating a new stage is to make it an exciting thing in itself." Again, it was Robert Edmund Jones who wrote that in *The Dramatic Imagination* those many years ago. Every great performance I can remember took place in a space that was special. You knew it when you walked in. And sometimes, at least, the play seemed so very easy to unveil there. One thing is certain, such a space would not disappear when the play begins, nor would our fellow viewers.

How do we develop new architectural models? First, we gain better experiences connecting with our audiences. Better experiences at making the event memorable, at building on a special time. Some of those opportunities may come as unexpected gifts, ones that initially appear in unlikely disguises. We have only to be alert to the possibilities, to have the courage to choose what our best instincts suggest, to remember what opportunity or accident or good fortune makes possible, applying the insight to our next effort. Step by step.

I am reminded of one of those unlikely gifts I came to love, a space that became magical. A space where performances were so memorable even I—even now—can but shake my head at their impact despite what seemed like overwhelming limitations. No, it was not the ideal theatre. Not even one of the ideal theatres. But it was where I learned an unforgettable lesson. If you are searching for a starting place, it suggests a possibility for nearly every director who can bring together an audience.

The building was on the town square facing a nineteenth-century country courthouse in a Midwest town of three thousand people. It was once home for a nineteenth-century furniture maker and funeral parlor—a logical combination at the time. When we found it, we were looking for a rain space for our outdoor theatre. A place where we could bring an audience determined to see a piece about Lincoln even in one of those Illinois downpours that were sure to come—sometime in July. Our theatre was in a state park only a couple of miles away, so it wasn't difficult to get that audience to drive the few additional miles when it became clear there would be no outdoor performance that night. Our alternative theatre was better known as the senior citizen center, and every weekday at noon many of the town's seniors gathered for lunch on the second floor. It had a simple décor, but polished hardwood floors and embossed tin ceilings were not unattractive, and when you took the central staircase up to the third floor you were suddenly aware of a long rectangular room with a huge picture window at one end and restrooms well beyond the stairway railings at the other. Track lighting lined the walls.

We were introduced to the space by Bud Faith, a retired postman, who had become one of our most valued volunteers. Yes, he ate lunch there everyday. And with his help, for eight years it became our "rain space."

We would load up our vehicles with an eight- by twelve-foot image of Lincoln that came to stand at one end of the space, a truckload of smaller props, and wardrobes filled with costumes. In an hour or a little more we would have lined the walls with banners and posters, focused the lights, set up our sound equipment, and been ready for an audience of seventy-five to one hundred people—on a few occasions, we crammed almost two hundred into the space. Here was the key: folding chairs were arranged to provide three clear playing spaces with aisles that allowed the actors to move through the audience in an almost endless set of patterns. They appeared behind and through the audience, coming from all directions. An occasional small platform was moved in place when we needed the extra height, but the cinematic script and constantly changing scene meant that everyone at one time had the best seat in the house—this last a principle I had come to believe in early in my directing career. Yes, with effort, a director can make almost any seat the best seat for a brief period of time. A special seat offering its own unique experience.

Here, no seat was ever more than four rows deep, and even when you were in the last of those four rows, something was usually happening in the aisle beside you or the one just behind. Fifteen actors were in that space doing something all the time, even if it was only lying at (on?) your feet. There was music, an original score, but many of the melodies were well-known civil war songs, and more than a few in the audience might be heard singing softly along with the cast when the time came. The central stairwell provided for the most dramatic entrances; a fire-escape exit in a rear corner—just beyond the rest rooms— allowed actors to slip out of the space, go down a floor, and get ready for their next appearance if they were to make the big entrance up the stairs. But mostly, they just stayed there—with their audience. Even their costume changes were made behind screens in the room's corners.

Compared with our scheduled performances, it was what Peter Brook called "The Rough Theatre." And—for us—I think it did save the day, just as Brook says is often the case.

Lincoln himself had done the original survey for the town, and as the rain beat against the windows we looked out on the courthouse where many of his papers had been found tucked away in corners from the time he had lawyered as part of the Eighth Judicial Circuit.

I loved arranging those chairs, projecting whatever the audience size for that night might demand, leaving a niche here, an aisle there, grouping five seats together in one cluster, a section of four pairs where the barrels were to be placed or the "campfire" built. My cast knew it was something I took very seriously. We knew that the audiences who came seemed always grateful to have had a chance to get a little closer to the life in that small Midwest town. Our outdoor theatre was much more impressive, of course. It made possible complex choreography only hinted at here, but we never heard anyone complain that they had had to settle for a shadow of the "real" production. Yes, they would be back, they said, "to see it on a clear summer night—on the big stage." But whether they were from London or Kansas City, they knew this was a pretty unique experience Bud Faith and his senior citizens had made possible. It was a little like creating a tent under the dining room table, I suppose, being protected here from the storms raging out the window and getting a dose of American history. And as much as I love stages with complex platforming as a tool for moving from one time and place to another, arranging those chairs could be magic.

It was a powerful lesson. About space and the connections we can sometimes make when the place is special and you find a way to have the actors and the audience share time together. Really share.

Pretty simple when you get it right.

Epilogue:

Possible? Yes, of course. Absolutely! If we can begin. If we can take the first steps and are willing to get in touch with the difference. And then keep at it. Again and again.

And again....

These seven possibilities cover a lot of territory. They require change. Eventually, to have consistently great theatre, enormous change. Change in many, many habits and many long-established systems. Fundamental changes. Fundamental changes in the way we think things must be done.

Will we save the living theatre?

Maybe.

First, we need to believe it worth saving.

I *know* a far better theatre is possible. I suspect most who read this far will agree. Even if you seldom see it, I suspect you will agree. The question is, how important could the living theatre—the living theatre at its very best—be to twenty-first century America? How important could it be to the community you care about most?

135

Yes, the finances are difficult. And certainly there is a practical reality that jumps into the path of all Don Quixotes. Yes, it's tough to find the starting place. The need for the right people, the right community, the right building, the right script, the right equipment—any one of these missing links can cause you to throw up your hands. And if you are starting from scratch and have none of the above, the challenge is awesome. Only the foolhearted or the very young dare begin under such circumstances. And that, in fact, is how most theatres have started. Naïvely, with little insight into what lies ahead. Those very few who have held on have almost always been the recipients of a lightning strike of good fortune. The question is, What have we learned from either our good luck or our succumbing to what, in retrospect, too often seems like the inevitable? Obviously, I have argued we haven't learned as much as we need to.

This book has grown out of a deep personal belief: If we trust that the living theatre—at its best—has something incredibly valuable to offer its community, that community may well discover it won't let it go.

Whether it's a small town or a nation, that understanding has seldom had much currency in America, and reversing our dismissal of this Promethean gift certainly won't happen overnight. We seem to be on the eve of abandoning newspapers as an indispensable tool and comfort at the start of the day. Does the success of the Web mean libraries are doomed? Is the feel of turning a page to go the way of the curtain's going up on the performance? Maybe.

But somewhere in our love and need for museums and parks, churches and concerts is a deep-rooted need to come together to share the search for better understanding, to celebrate our best efforts, to mourn our deepest losses, to know who we are, where we have been, and where we are headed. That, I believe, hasn't changed—and won't. I saw it recently when I first visited the fountain in Chicago's Millennium Park, a shallow concrete rectangle flanked by two projection towers with changing faces that smiled and frowned and spouted water before us. Where children and adults rushed in to splash and dance and laugh as they were reminded that there was a place for them among the continuously building and rebuilding of skyscrapers on the lakefront. A place where their own faces matched up well with those water-spouting projected images as if proving they too were part of this enormous, sometimes cruel and impersonal city.

Cell phone users or not, Web addicts or not, I believe we still need to dance in the water, laughing and crying together as we watch the faces around us tell us about themselves and their families and their jobs and their dreams and their sorrows. Tell us about *us*.

The need is in our genes.

And if the theatre—the living theatre—isn't saved, isn't what it might be, our genes keep looking for it. Looking somewhere. Call it religion or the Rolling Stones in concert or stock car races or bingo, we come together looking to see who we are and where we are going.

If the living theatre wants to survive, it has to get a lot better at developing its system for sharing our lives and histories and dreams. We can create, but we must learn to create better *together*. Like much we do in America, the theatre has prized independence more than interdependence, has celebrated winners, not realizing that learning together, changing places in the circle, may be more important than training a few to be first in crossing our finish lines.

Maybe it was by writing this book that I came closest to convincing myself how lucky I have been in my career. I did not become rich nor terribly well-known, although we—my theatre and I—had our moments and certainly our believers. What I *can* say is that I remain convinced ours was an accomplishment of note. We gave voice to experiences that urgently needed airing, struggles that were known but had too easily been taken for granted. And we did it in a place that gave us what we needed: courage. Courage to dare say, to ourselves and others, "What we are doing is important. Truly important."

On an Illinois State Historic Site with a restored village where Lincoln once lived, near a little Midwest town he surveyed, some twenty miles from the Lincoln Home and the Old State Capitol, where he gave his "house divided" speech and where his body lay in state when he was brought home, I learned a great deal. By creating a theatre there, by sustaining it for twenty years, I learned about people. About life. About the theatre.

I am convinced the theatre's real search is for ways to bring together changing sensibilities and universal experiences. Changing sensibilities conditioned today, in great part, by continuing exposure to twenty-first century technologies in the shadow of those near-eternal, universal experiences that haven't changed significantly in the years from the Greeks through the Elizabethans to the present day.

I believe we have too often seen our choices as black and white. We have been too concerned with what *most* expect—most actors, most designers, most playwrights, most audience members, most producers. We suffer from being specialists who protect our very limited interests. Preoccupied with movement for the actor, with diction or dialects, with choreography or lighting projections, we have left it to somebody else to tend to the theatre's core. We are fund-raisers and audience developers who seldom concern ourselves with the bone-deep possibilities of an art whose historic power started with explorations of the human soul, an art that offers us an unparalleled opportunity for connecting with one another.

Directors are often seen as the villains in unsuccessful theatre. More than one writer has addressed the very real issue of an actor's difficulty in working under a director who leads her away from her potentially best effort, who creates obstacles to her creativity. Such concerns are often justified.

The director's central role in shaping a production is seldom well understood by those outside the process. But it is important to remember that few successful leaders can lead those who resist, who do not have a shared belief in the mission. Even as I

have focused on the system—a system for collective creations—
it is clear that my own bias expects the director to play a central
role. But it should also be clear that the issues raised here cannot
be the concern of the director alone. Because a director interacts
with so many different people, he has the possibility of being
overrun by insecure contributors from many directions—collaborators who fear you are creating more work, more difficult
work, less successful work for them. Even established collaborators—sometimes especially established collaborators—can be
among the most conservative. Why? If you change, you will
be challenging the system. Every established system evolves by
serving its stakeholders in a tolerated way. Some may grumble,
even protest, but if they continue to be part of the system, they
are served by it in at least some significant way.

My intent here has been to try to write for those who have
been unwilling or unable to explore other possibilities—but
who somehow recognize there must be a better way. A more significant way. A different direction. My intent has been to write
for them, whatever their role in a collective system for creating
living theatre.

I have spent much of my life in the academic theatre. In the
early years of that work I longed for a professional company. In
the second half of that work, I did everything I could imagine
to avoid ours becoming a professional company. In retrospect,
I realize I was extremely fortunate in all three phases of my
career: I left graduate school, accepting a job in a small, liberal
arts college where I didn't have to fit into someone else's program. As much of a struggle as it sometimes was, I was free to
take that program where my studies had suggested the potential lay. Students, administrative officials, and audiences began
to respond in ways that seem even more amazing now than they
did at the time.

I left there eager for the stimulation of more experienced
theatre colleagues and eager to see what might be possible in
one of the largest performance arts centers in the country—a
facility under construction, but one where I might play a role

in shaping its final form. At that university I had a chance to work with equipment and in theatres that were, and for many still are, the envy of theatre people everywhere. I learned from those shops and equipment and colleagues. I learned not only what was possible when collaborators are in agreement, but what struggles can ensue when would-be collaborators are in basic conflict over what we are doing and where we are headed.

And, in the last phase of my work, 1976, the bicentennial year, gave me a chance to start my own company. Not just a theatre, but a theatre growing out of a recognition of the potential in stories from our American experience. Personal stories. Stories that were in our bones.

It was quite a ride.

Since retiring, I have been content to write, to enjoy my new life in Southern California, and most of all to enjoy my relationships with my wife, children, grandchildren, and friends and to see parts of the world I had not expected to see.

That this book was begun at all was somewhat of a surprise to me. That it was as challenging to write as it became—another surprise. For it is one thing to say, "Yes, these are things I know." It is another to try to find what might be valuable to someone else. Especially if the sharing is in a culture where little confirms the importance of the issues you raise.

But these last eight years have been especially trying for many of us in America and I suppose, in some respect, we have all scratched the earth in whatever way our pasts made possible, trying to plant a seed that might give us some shade. Might give us a tree to climb where we can see over the horizon.

I am finishing this effort at an amazing time. The inauguration of Barack Obama, the first black American to be elected president of the United States, will take place on the Capitol steps in Washington, D.C....tomorrow! With it: hope.

Hope.

Even in the midst of calamity, we have all felt it—or nearly all of us.

So...how can I possibly believe the theatre cannot do better? Don't we all have "Yes We Can!" ringing in our ears? No, I haven't heard a single voice—not even my own—say the resurrection of the theatre should be given high priority in the face of the issues demanding our attention. But, compared with the challenge to create a healthy economy, to find peace in the Middle East, to extract our forces from Iraq and Afghanistan, to make health care and equal rights available and assured for all...it seems simple.

Can we begin? I'd like to think we can.

The seven possibilities outlined here are not really so impossible, after all. At least taking those first small steps forward with each of them is not so impossible. What might stop us? Whatever the details of the resistance, I suspect most arguments could be distilled to one: cost. "The financial realities don't make it practical." But art is not practical any more than life is practical. And don't we find a way if we want something badly enough? If we can imagine it, if we can see the possibilities? For a debt-ridden nation, isn't it amazing that hundreds of thousands—millions—came to Washington to be part of the inaugural event? Part of the inauguration of the forty-fourth president of the United States of America?

And if you watched the concert of celebration on the steps of the Lincoln Memorial with those throngs stretched out before the performers, can you doubt the arts have something to tell us about ourselves? About who we are and what is possible? If you watched all those icons and choruses—those witnesses— borrow from our past as they pointed us toward our future, do you doubt we have something to sing about? Do you doubt our audiences have something to share with us and we with them?

I believe we can have a great theatre, a valued theatre, if we can see new possibilities. If we are willing to make significant changes in the way we connect with one another as we try to get there.

Isn't that always true? Hasn't it been true for every impossible thing we've somehow accomplished? How good could it be—this living theatre?

. . . .

How good do we want it to be?

———————

"Now, there are some who question the scale of our ambitions—who suggest that our system cannot tolerate too many big plans.
Their memories are short.
For they have forgotten what this country has already done;
what free men and women can achieve
when imagination is joined to common purpose,
and necessity to courage."
—Barack Obama
Presidential Inaugural Address,
January 20, 2009

About the Author

John Ahart has had a long and distinguished career in the American theatre. *A Different Direction* is the product of his forty-one years of experience as director, playwright, designer, and teacher.

At the University of Illinois he supervised the graduate directors' workshop and later headed the MFA directing program for much of his thirty-two-year tenure, directing a wide range of major works at the Krannert Center for the Performing Arts.

His original production, *Head of State*, was performed at the Kennedy Center as part of the American College Theatre Festival and led to the creation of a new theatre company which the press came to call "...a national treasure." He was founding and artistic director of that company, The Great American People Show, performing at New Salem, Illinois, for twenty years, beginning in the bicentennial year, 1976. Under his direction, GAPS was the first theatre to win the Illinois Governor's Arts Award, presenting more than one thousand performances of original works drawn from American history. It became Illinois' state theatre and was a model for projects developed by the Illinois Humanities Council and the National Endowment for the Humanities.

Since his retirement, he has resided in Southern California, where he has devoted his time to writing. His *Director's Eye* has become a popular directing text, called by one critic, "...[one of the two] finest books ever written about the art of directing." *A Different Direction* brings together Ahart's insight gained through four decades of practical experience creating original works, directing theatre classics from Brecht to Beckett to Shakespeare, using and developing nontraditional theatre spaces, and building and sustaining a theatre company that gave voice to Americans, spanning 160 years of our history.

Ahart holds a BA from Marietta College, an MA from the University of Illinois, and a PhD from the University of Minnesota.